Her Hand in Marriage

Rebecca Lange

Published by Rebecca Lange Books, 2021.

HER HAND IN MARRIAGE

First edition. December 11, 2021.

Copyright © 2021 Rebecca Lange.

ISBN: 979-8233272370

Written by Rebecca Lange.

Table of Contents

...for everyone who thinks writing a book is easy - Is it?
Then where is your book?

HER HAND IN MARRIAGE

First edition. December 11, 2021.

Second edition. January 2026.

Copyright © 2026 Rebecca Lange.

Prologue

London, England,
Sept. 1, 1813

Lord Kenneth Mulligan,
Earl of Adare
Limerick, Ireland

Kind Sir,

I am pleased to inform you that I am prepared to accept your proposal, provided certain conditions are observed. My parents' dearest wish has ever been that our estate remain within the family, and a marriage between you and our youngest daughter, Sophie Aoife, would honor both their wish and our agreement.

My wife, however, cannot consent to your proposal as originally written and insists that her requests be included as terms of final acceptance:

1. The engagement between you and our daughter may not be publicly announced until after her nineteenth birthday.
2. The wedding must take place on Christmas Eve, in accordance with a long-standing family tradition which must be preserved.

For your convenience, I enclose the contract, duly signed and sealed, with these conditions incorporated. Should you find these terms agreeable, we beg your swift confirmation and return of the agreement so that the pact may be finalized and made official.

Yours most respectfully,
Albert Theodore Everton

Prologue

London, England,
Sept. 1, 1813

Lord Kenneth Mulligan,
Earl of Adare
Limerick, Ireland

Kind Sir,

I am pleased to inform you that I am prepared to accept your proposal, provided certain conditions are observed. My parents' dearest wish has ever been that our estate remain within the family, and a marriage between you and our youngest daughter, Sophie Aoife, would honor both their wish and our agreement.

My wife, however, cannot consent to your proposal as originally written and insists that her requests be included as terms of final acceptance:

1. The engagement between you and our daughter may not be publicly announced until after her nineteenth birthday.
2. The wedding must take place on Christmas Eve, in accordance with a long-standing family tradition which must be preserved.

For your convenience, I enclose the contract, duly signed and *sealed, with these conditions incorporated. Should you find these terms agreeable, we beg your swift confirmation and return of the agreement so that the pact may be finalized and made official.*

Yours most respectfully,

Albert Theodore Everton

1

The Earl's Command

"I am going for a walk, Grandmama."

"Do that, but please take Brian or Thomas with you."

"I will be fine, Grandmama. I won't be going far, and Brian and Thomas are always awkward around me. They never speak."

Augusta's lips curved into a faint smile, though she tried not to show too much amusement. She was hardly surprised that the servants remained tongue-tied in Sophie's presence. Her granddaughter possessed a striking beauty, full of life and energy, but it was coupled with a boldness of spirit that unsettled those unaccustomed to such frankness. Sophie spoke her mind freely, often without hesitation, and the quiet, deferential servants were easily discomposed by her manner.

Of course, the girl had not lived under their roof for long. Time, Augusta told herself, would soften the awkwardness. The servants would grow used to Sophie's ways, though it might take patience on both sides.

Sophie had been entrusted to their care only after the sudden and devastating death of her parents. Even now, months later, the cause of their passing remained shrouded in mystery. Augusta often wondered if her granddaughter knew more than she let on, though she suspected the girl was as much in the dark as they.

Her son Albert—dear, foolish Albert—had always been secretive, guarding family matters too closely. It was unlikely he had ever spoken openly with his daughter about her mother's kin. Indeed, no one within the household was permitted to mention her daughter-in-law's family.

That silence weighed heavy, unyielding as stone. The Everton line bore the mingling of nobility and common blood. Her husband's grandfather, after leaving Cambridge, had chosen medicine over rank and married a commoner. He worked tirelessly as a physician until his father's death compelled him to assume the barony. From that point forward, each son had followed the same course—devoting himself to the practice of healing rather than the privileges of birth. Even Albert had carried on the tradition, setting aside the trappings of nobility for a physician's calling.

Augusta stood at the window, her gaze following Sophie as the girl stepped into the bracing air. The season had turned bitter. The wind swept fiercely across the open fields and tore through the village lanes. Pulling her shawl more tightly about her shoulders, Augusta predicted that Sophie, ever sensible despite her spirited nature, would seek shelter in the forest rather than endure the raw gusts along the open path.

"Darling," came her husband's voice from behind. Edwin Everton crossed the hall with his usual briskness, his hand resting briefly on the doorframe. "Please send Sophie to me. I need to speak with her."

"She just left," Augusta called, turning to him. "She went for a walk."

"She did?" He joined her at the window, and together they

watched their granddaughter's slim figure retreat, dwindling against the russet backdrop of the autumn woods until she vanished into the gathering shadows.

"What did you wish to discuss with her?" Augusta asked at last. Edwin's sigh was heavy, burdened with many sleepless nights.

"I have received another letter from Lord Mulligan. His plans for the engagement are growing ever more elaborate. I tried to explain we cannot indulge such extravagance, but he insists upon every point agreed with Albert. I fear, Augusta, we shall be forced to draw upon Sophie's dowry to meet his demands."

Augusta's jaw tightened, her fingers clenching the folds of her gown. "I wish our son had never consented to such a reckless agreement with the Earl of Adare. Sophie appears content for the moment—because she loves this land, our home, our heritage—but soon she will feel the chains of such an arrangement. And when that day comes, she will know she is trapped."

Edwin nodded gravely. "She has had little contact with Lord Mulligan thus far. But once their engagement is made public, the pressure upon her will increase. He will demand her attention, her compliance, and he will not stop pressing. I know our Sophie—her temper, her pride. His forcefulness may well backfire."

"And if she should refuse him?" Augusta's voice was low, edged with desperation. "Do we have any power to release her from this union?"

Her husband shook his head, the answer as bitter as gall. "None. Albert bound her future with ink and seal. The contract is ironclad, and Sophie is not yet of age. Mulligan paid off all of Albert's debts, and by doing so, secured not only this estate but our livelihoods. If Sophie dares resist, we lose everything. And Mulligan is not a man to shrink from force. He would compel her if need be." Edwin paused, his shoulders sagging.

"Yet knowing Sophie, she would never allow us to suffer such loss. Her pride would compel her to sacrifice herself rather than see our home and name destroyed."

Augusta's composure faltered. Anger flared hot through her sorrow. "Albert was a fool," she hissed, her voice sharp with long-suppressed bitterness. "He sold his daughter's freedom to a man we hardly know, bartering her future for the sake of his own indulgences—his debts, his obsessions, his endless recklessness."

"Yes," Edwin murmured, his eyes still fixed upon the darkened trees where their granddaughter had vanished. "And now it is Sophie who must pay the price for her father's sins."

Sophie delighted in the crisp bite of the air as she walked, her cheeks flushed with the chill, her breath rising in soft clouds. Autumn had painted the forest in brilliance that stole her breath—a riot of crimson, gold, and russet leaves shimmering in the afternoon light. The wind carried the mingled scents of wood smoke and earth, as though the season itself whispered secrets of change and wonder.

She drew in a deep breath, savoring the freshness, and spun in a sudden twirl, her skirts fanning around her as laughter bubbled from her lips. For the first time in days, she felt unburdened—almost free.

The joyous sound of barking broke her reverie. Sophie turned, her smile widening as her faithful companions bounded toward her—her own collie, Cleo, and her grandfather's spirited Irish setter, Celeste. Their presence warmed her heart, though their indignant grunts made their disapproval clear.

"I know, I know," Sophie laughed, crouching to gather them close. She rubbed their silky heads, pressing her face into Cleo's ruff. "Forgive me for slipping away without you. I feared Grandmama would not let me go alone if I didn't hurry out of the house."

Cleo rewarded her with a wet lick across the cheek, while Celeste, brimming with joy, launched herself into Sophie's arms and knocked her clean to the ground. Sophie landed amid the carpet of fallen leaves, her giggles echoing through the trees until they spilled into unrestrained, heartfelt laughter.

"Celeste, you naughty girl!" she scolded fondly, brushing stray curls from her face as she sat up. "You know you're not supposed to do that. Grandfather is terribly strict about such behavior."

Celeste barked in what sounded suspiciously like defiance before bounding off again. Both dogs tore through the undergrowth in a blur of fur and delight, weaving between the trees as though chasing the wind itself. Sophie rose, shaking leaves from her skirts, her heart lighter than it had been in a long while.

But in the next instant, the atmosphere shifted. The dogs halted abruptly, bodies taut, ears pricked. Their carefree chase ended in a heartbeat. Hackles bristling, they rushed back to Sophie's side, a low, guttural growl rising in their throats.

Sophie froze, alarm prickling through her chest. Something, or someone, was approaching. And whatever it was, Cleo and Celeste did not welcome it as friend.

Just as Sophie debated whether she ought to turn back toward the safety of home, the distant rattle of wheels reached her ears. A carriage rolled into view along the narrow path, its wheels crunching over fallen leaves. The driver drew the horses to a halt beside her, and two figures stepped down.

Sophie stiffened at once. She knew them, Herbert Boyle and Declan Moore, long-serving men in the household of the Earl of Adare. Their presence here was no chance encounter.

"Miss Everton," Boyle said smoothly, though the curl of his lip betrayed disdain. "How fortunate to find you here alone. The Earl of Adare has sent us to fetch you. He expects your company at once, to discuss the particulars of your upcoming engagement celebration."

Sophie inclined her head with practiced politeness, though her dogs bristled and growled at her side.

"Mr. Boyle. Mr. Moore," she greeted, her tone calm, her smile strained. "It is... good to see you again. Yet if Lord Mulligan wishes to speak with me, I must ask—why does he not come himself?"

Boyle's mouth twisted into a humorless grin. "His Lordship is a busy man, Miss Everton. He cannot simply rise and leave whenever the mood strikes. That is why he sends us."

Sophie lifted a brow, brushing a lock of windblown hair from her shoulder with deliberate grace.

"And yet he expects me to abandon my own plans at a moment's notice? Forgive me, gentlemen, but I must decline. I am due to return shortly to my grandparents. I cannot keep them waiting."

Boyle stepped closer, boots crunching over the frosted leaves—only to stop short as Cleo and Celeste lunged forward, lips drawn back, their growls deepening into feral warning. The hair along their spines stood rigid, their teeth bared, every muscle coiled as though ready to spring.

The servant faltered, his expression hardening as he shifted his glare from the dogs to Sophie.

"You appear to be under the mistaken impression that you have a choice in the matter," he said coldly. "When the Earl of Adare wishes to see someone, it is not a request. It is an order. You will come with us—now."

The polite veneer Sophie had worn shattered. Her chin lifted, her blue eyes blazing with fire.

"I do not take orders from anyone," she said, her voice sharp as steel. "If Lord Mulligan has urgent business with me, he is welcome to call upon me at my family's estate. There, he may speak with me under my roof."

Boyle's smirk returned, uglier this time. "That estate is not yours anymore, Miss Everton. The Earl owns it, and he may ask you to leave it at a moment's notice."

A shock like ice ran through Sophie's veins, though she forced her features to remain composed. She would not give them the satisfaction of seeing her falter. With cool determination, she met his gaze, her loathing clear.

She had never trusted these men—never liked them. Their manners were coarse, their words laced with contempt, and their faces bore the hardness of cruelty. Herbert Boyle, in particular, had always unsettled her. His jet-black hair framed piercing green eyes, but it was the jagged scar slashing across his left cheek that lent him a sinister air.

Now, as he dared another step forward, the dogs surged with fury, their growls erupting like thunder. Boyle hesitated—uncertainty flickering across his face for the first time

Sophie's temper flared, hot and unyielding. How dare this

man—the man she was expected to marry—presume to command her as though she were a servant at his beck and call? Fury burned through her chest, mingling with the sharp sting of betrayal.

And what was this talk of the estate? The words clawed at her heart. Could it be true? Was that why her father, on his deathbed, had pressed her so fiercely to promise obedience to Lord Mulligan? Had he bartered away their beloved home, her home, without a word to her? Had he bound her future to a man she scarcely knew, wagering her happiness against debts she had never been told existed? The thought made her stomach turn.

But Sophie would not cower. She lifted her chin high, defiance flashing in her blue eyes.

"Lord Mulligan may do as he wishes," she declared, her voice ringing with cold clarity. "If he believes Beech Tree Hall is not enough for him, then so be it. I will not be his prisoner. I would sooner earn my bread as a governess than bow to such arrogance."

Both Boyle and Moore drew sharp breaths, startled into silence. Their eyes darted over her slight frame, as though struggling to reconcile the delicate young woman before them with the steel lacing her words. Sophie had met them only twice before, but it was plain that neither had expected such fire from her.

Boyle's sneer returned. Ignoring the snarling dogs, he lunged forward and seized Sophie's arm in his rough grip. But he had scarcely laid hold of her when Cleo and Celeste erupted in fury. With a chorus of savage growls, they hurled themselves at him, sinking their teeth into the heavy fabric of his coat and dragging him hard to the ground.

Sophie gasped, stumbling back as chaos erupted before her

eyes. The guttural sounds rumbling in her dogs' throats were no longer mere warnings, they were promises of violence. One wrong move, and Boyle's flesh would pay the price. For the briefest instant, fear stabbed through her—not for herself, but for her loyal companions. What would happen to them if they unleashed their full wrath?

The truth struck her like ice. This was no polite errand, no simple summons on the earl's behalf. They had been sent to force her into that carriage. This was an attempt to take her against her will—to kidnap her.

Declan Moore, keeping his distance from the snapping dogs, fixed Sophie with a glare as cold as death. His voice was low, edged with menace.

"I recommend you come willingly, Sophie. The Earl of Adare is not a patient man, and he will act accordingly."

Her eyes narrowed, blazing with contempt. "I am Miss Everton to you," she retorted, each word sharp as a blade. "And you may carry whatever tale you please back to Lord Mulligan—but know this: when next I see him, he will learn how you dared to lay hands upon me, and how you threatened me in his name."

Moore's expression twisted with disgust. He raked a hand through his thick, flaming-red hair, revealing more of his battered features: a crooked nose long since broken, and gaps where teeth were missing. His scoff brimmed with loathing, but before he could lose another insult, movement on the path stilled every tongue.

Three rugged men emerged from the forest shadows, their horses at their heels. Their arrival was sudden, almost startling.

Sophie realized with a jolt that she had been so consumed by her quarrel with the earl's servants she had failed to hear them approach.

Cleo and Celeste turned their fury on the newcomers, hackles raised—until, sensing no threat, they eased back. Boyle, on the other hand, scrambled awkwardly to his feet, tearing himself free of the dogs' grip and stumbling a step away from Sophie, his bravado dimmed in the face of this unexpected company.

One of the newcomers stepped forward, his presence commanding the path as naturally as sunlight breaking through clouds. Sophie's breath caught as she regarded him from the corner of her eye. He was striking—tall and broad-shouldered, with tafia-brown hair that gleamed lighter where the light touched it.

Though his expression was stern, there was something unmistakable beneath it: a quiet strength, a steadiness, and even a flicker of compassion that stood in sharp contrast to the malice of the men who had accosted her.

His voice, deep and unwavering, carried authority. "I suggest you return to your master at once and leave the young lady alone. I daresay Lord Mulligan will not be pleased when he learns how you have conducted yourselves in his name."

Herbert Boyle let out a harsh laugh, though his eyes betrayed a flash of unease. "It is none of your concern how we treat her. And let me be plain, she is no lady. If you have come here to play the gallant hero, you waste both your time and your breath. The young mistress is already promised to the earl, and nothing you do will change that." His words dripped with disdain, his sneer deepening as he spoke.

2

When Nobility Meets Defiance

Declan Moore bristled, his voice cutting like a whip. "And who are you, exactly? I do not recall ever seeing your face in these parts before."

The handsome stranger held his ground. "We have come from Limerick."

"Well then," Boyle shot back, his voice rising with anger, "I suggest you return there at once. You are not welcome here." His fists tightened at his sides, his temper slipping beyond control.

"Watch your tone, servant," one of the other newcomers growled, stepping forward. His piercing blue eyes blazed, and his hand fell deliberately to the hilt of his sword. "Another word of insolence, and you may well find yourself in the dungeon."

Boyle and Moore burst into mocking laughter, the sound coarse and grating against the stillness of the wood.

"The dungeon, is it?" Moore sneered. "Feeling rather important, are we? And what might your occupation be, sir? A groundskeeper? A stable master?"

Before the man could reply, the third of the newcomers advanced. He carried himself with calm assurance, his dark hair streaked with silver at the temples. His voice, controlled and steady, cut cleanly through the mockery.

"Mr. Seamus Farrell," he announced evenly, gesturing toward the younger man, "is first footman to the Duke of Limerick."

For a moment, Boyle and Moore faltered. Their laughter died on their lips, leaving a tense silence hanging in the air. Then Boyle, his voice thinner than before, demanded, "And you are?"

The older man's eyes gleamed with quiet authority as he stepped closer.

"Rafferty McMahon. Steward and personal protector of His Grace. And since you seem determined to court disgrace, allow me to spare you the trouble of further folly." He extended his hand toward the dark-haired man who had first spoken. "It is my honor to present our master—Lord Liam Ronan Walsh, Duke of Limerick."

The effect was immediate. Sophie's lips curved into a smile as she drank in the sight of the two servants' faces. Their bravado crumbled into shock, then into the humiliation of recognition. Whatever arrogance they had clung to dissolved. Without a word, they bowed their heads in grudging deference.

"You may leave now," Rafferty McMahon continued, his voice ringing with finality. "But rest assured, your conduct here will be reported to your master without omission."

Boyle and Moore exchanged a dark glance before turning away, their jaws set tight. As they passed the carriage, Boyle shoved the driver roughly against the wheel, punishing him for the faint smirk of amusement lingering on his lips.

Liam's gaze lingered on Sophie as the carriage rumbled out of sight. Relief softened her features at last, the tightness in her shoulders melting as though a great weight had been lifted. He felt a spark of admiration for the young woman who had stood her ground so fiercely, yet who now seemed suddenly fragile in the fading light of the forest. Offering her a warm, steady look, he hoped to reassure her further.

Sophie dipped into a graceful curtsy, but before she could finish, Liam stepped forward and gently caught her hand. With a firm yet courteous tug, he drew her upright again.

"There is no need for such formalities out here in the forest," he said, his voice low and intent, his dark eyes fixed upon her face. A delicate flush rose in her cheeks, painting them a soft pink that deepened under his regard. "I trust it was in your interest that we intervened?"

"It was indeed, Your Grace," Sophie replied, her tone composed though gratitude glimmered in her eyes. "I thank you for rescuing me from those impertinent men."

"They were far out of line, Miss Everton," Rafferty interjected, his voice edged with indignation as he glanced at his master. "That is no way to address, let alone handle, a lady."

Sophie gave a short laugh—light, touched with irony. "Oh, they were right about one thing. I am not a lady."

"Perhaps not in the sense of rank and title," Liam countered gently, charmed by both her wit and her candor. "But that does not make you any less of a lady in the truest sense of the word."

Her lips parted slightly at his words, but before she could respond, she seemed to register what Mr. McMahon had called her. She blinked in surprise.

"Wait—how do you know my name? I have not lived here long enough to be recognized by strangers." Her expression was one of genuine confusion. Rafferty's grin spread wide.

"Are you not the granddaughter of Baron Everton?"

"I am," Sophie admitted cautiously. "But as I said, I only recently came to live here."

"As steward to His Grace," Rafferty replied smoothly, "it is my duty to know what happens within the villages of Limerick. And that, Miss Everton, includes the arrival of new residents."

Sophie exhaled softly, muttering under her breath, "And he just happens to have memorized every female face he's met..." Her eyes flicked skyward, caught between disbelief and embarrassment. Unbeknownst to her, the three men heard her perfectly well.

Seamus turned his head quickly to hide the grin tugging at his lips, while both Rafferty and Liam gave a brief cough to smother their amusement. With remarkable composure, Rafferty spoke in an even tone.

"Not every female face, my dear Miss Everton," he said, his eyes alight with mischief, "but I do recognize the ladies I have never seen before." His gaze lingered on her, watchful and eager, and just as he anticipated, her cheeks flamed a deep scarlet.

Liam's lips curved into a smile he could not quite suppress, his eyes drinking in the sight of her fluster.

"Forgive me," Sophie stammered, lowering her gaze. "I did not mean to be disrespectful."

"Don't trouble yourself, Miss Everton," Liam said gently. His voice carried warmth, his dark eyes steady on her face. "Rafferty was merely teasing."

Encouraged by his kindness, she lifted her gaze again, the color in her cheeks softening.

"It wasn't disrespectful at all," Rafferty assured her, inclining his head. "In truth, I would have wondered the same thing if a stranger had called me by name. And besides, your accent gave you away. We don't often have young ladies come from England to settle in these parts."

Her shoulders eased, the tension in her features melting away. The bright blush faded, leaving behind a gentler warmth in her expression. Liam studied her quietly, fascinated by how quickly her composure returned—how swiftly her spirit shone through once she no longer felt under scrutiny.

"I hope it isn't too forward of me," Sophie ventured, curiosity bright in her eyes, "but what brings you here to Adare?"

"Not forward at all," Liam replied with an easy smile. "I am touring the villages of Limerick to ensure all is in order—that servants and workers are treated justly. Word has reached us that some among the nobility have shown cruelty, even malice, toward those in their employ. His Majesty wishes to be kept informed of every such matter."

Sophie's eyes widened slightly, the blue in them brightening with interest. "That is very kind of the king," she said softly, admiration warming her tone.

Liam found it suddenly difficult to look away. The honesty in her expression, the light dancing in her eyes, held him fast. At length, he cleared his throat.

"We must continue our journey, but... may we call upon you this evening?"

A crimson blush stole once again across Sophie's cheeks. "Oh," she murmured with hesitation, "I—I am not certain."

"You already have plans?" Liam asked, tilting his head.

"My grandparents have invited our neighbors for supper," she explained.

"Then perhaps tomorrow?"

"It is not the timing," Sophie said quickly, her eyes darting up to meet his before dropping again. "I only mean... I am sure you must have other duties, other places to be."

"Our mission occupies us during the day," Liam replied, his tone quietly persuasive.

"I see," Sophie answered, her lips curving into a polite smile though her eyes betrayed her unease. "Well then, we shall be honored to welcome you to our home."

"Wonderful," Liam exclaimed before she could change her mind. "Rafferty will escort you home now."

"Oh no, that won't be necessary," Sophie said hurriedly, glancing at Rafferty with something close to pleading. "Truly, I will be quite safe. Please do not trouble yourself."

Rafferty's expression, however, had already shifted. The ease in his features vanished, replaced by the steady, protective gaze of a man accustomed to duty.

"You don't wish to be seen with me?" he teased lightly, though his eyes held a quiet challenge.

Liam and Seamus lowered their heads, shoulders shaking as they struggled not to laugh, while Sophie's face turned from soft pink to a blazing red.

"N—no, of course not," she stammered, her voice faltering. She no longer dared look at him. "Why would you think such a thing?"

This time, Rafferty allowed himself a broad grin. "My dear young madam, after what just occurred with the earl's men, no gentleman could permit you to walk back alone."

"Rafferty is right," Liam said, his voice firm and steady. "A gentleman would never allow it."

"I only do not wish to inconvenience you," Sophie whispered.

"It is no inconvenience," Rafferty assured her in a tone that brooked no further protest. "So please, do not make yourself uneasy." And that, it seemed, ended the discussion.

Liam stepped closer, his hand closing gently around hers. "Until this evening," he said softly, his eyes lingering on her face longer than propriety allowed. Yet he knew, from the quiet amusement of Seamus and Rafferty behind him, that his thoughts were plain enough.

With a final nod, he and Seamus mounted their horses and turned down the path, leaving Rafferty to see her home.

As soon as the men disappeared into the trees, Rafferty offered Sophie his arm. The dogs growled at once, protective and unyielding, but Sophie hushed them with a soft command. After a pause, she slipped her hand beneath his arm, her eyes cast downward, avoiding his gaze.

Rafferty studied her with quiet concern. Why did she seem so hesitant, so shy? Was it fear of him—or something else entirely?

"Sophie, darling, where have you been? We were worried sick." Augusta Everton rushed forward the moment her granddaughter stepped through the doorway, gathering the young woman into her arms as though she might vanish again if she let go.

"There is no need to be alarmed, Grandmama," Sophie soothed, her voice gentler than her words. "I will explain in a moment why I was gone longer than I had planned."

Edwin Everton stepped closer, his expression grave. "And who is this gentleman with you, Sophie?"

Sophie straightened, a faint flush rising in her cheeks as she realized her oversight. "Oh, forgive me. Grandmama, Grandfather—this is Mr. Rafferty McMahon, steward to the Duke of Limerick."

The elderly couple exchanged startled glances, their concern sharpening at the name. Augusta's hand lingered protectively on Sophie's arm, while Edwin's brows knit in thought. Mr. McMahon inclined his head in a respectful bow before addressing her grandfather directly. His voice was calm and courteous, though a thread of urgency ran beneath it.

"Might I have a word with you in private, sir?"

Edwin gave a brief nod. Before following him, McMahon turned once more to Sophie, his steady gaze softening.

"I shall take my leave now. Until this evening, Miss Everton." A faint smile touched his lips before he accompanied Edwin down the corridor toward the study.

Augusta, still unsettled, slipped her arm through Sophie's and guided her into the drawing room. Once the door was closed, she turned on her granddaughter with a mixture of worry and affection etched upon her face.

"Now, child, tell me what has happened," she urged, pressing Sophie gently toward the settee. "I cannot say that I feel any easier knowing you returned in the company of the duke's steward. Are you in some kind of trouble?"

Sophie sat down, smoothing her skirts with deliberate calm,

though her eyes betrayed the turmoil she carried.

"I am well, Grandmama—truly. Please, sit with me, and I will tell you everything from the beginning."

"That is outrageous," Augusta snapped the moment Sophie finished recounting her encounter with Lord Mulligan's servants. Her cheeks flushed with indignation, her hands clenching in her lap. "Earl or not, he has no right to do such a thing."

"Do you think it was truly his command, Grandmama?" Sophie asked quickly, leaning forward with anxious eagerness. "Or did the servants act on their own, hoping to appear more important in their master's eyes?"

Augusta's shoulders lifted helplessly in a shrug. "I honestly do not know what to think, child. We know little of the earl. He moved here not long before you came to us, and his home before that was London. I cannot say what sort of man he truly is."

"I do not know him well either," Sophie admitted softly. "Father told me before his death that I was to be engaged to Lord Mulligan, but I have met him only a few times. He always seemed kind—every inch the gentleman." Her voice faltered as her gaze drifted. "And though I cannot deny that he is handsome, he is also thirteen years my senior."

The room fell into tense silence, the weight of her words pressing down until Sophie spoke again, her tone stronger, more resolute.

"If Lord Mulligan is not the man I believed him to be, then I do not want to marry him. Father made me promise to accept him as my husband, but surely even he did not know the man's true nature." She turned, her eyes searching her grandmother's face.

"Grandfather can stop him from pursuing me, can he not, Grandmama?"

Before Augusta could reply, Edwin appeared in the doorway. His expression was grave as he stepped into the room.

"I am afraid there is little I can do, Sophie. Your father signed a contract. According to its terms, Lord Mulligan purchased our land and estate and cleared Albert's debts. We are bound by his word, and I have no power to undo it."

Sophie's face drained of color, her lips parting in disbelief. "You cannot mean this. Father sold me to that man?" Her voice cracked. "But he always made it sound as though I still had a choice. Yes, he pressed me to promise, but he never told me the truth—that I had no say at all."

3

The Past Unveiled

Her grandparents exchanged a sorrowful glance before Edwin crossed the room and drew Sophie gently into his arms. His voice was heavy with regret.

"I am truly sorry, my dear. Our son made countless mistakes. We never knew the extent of his debts until it was too late. Each time he came to us, we gave what savings we could. But when most of our tenants moved away, our income collapsed, and we could no longer help him. It was then he confessed the full measure of his debts and warned us that we were all on the brink of ruin." He sighed, the sound weary and broken.

"Your grandmother and I tried to devise a plan, but it was useless. We were desperate, so when Albert told us he had found a way to preserve our estate, we believed him. We thought, foolishly, that he had saved us." Anger flared briefly in Edwin's eyes, hardening his tone.

"But he had already acted without our knowledge. He stole the important papers and deeds from my study during one of his visits. Without them, we had no legal claim to the property. And only after the deed was done did he inform us—by letter, no less—that he had signed a binding contract. Lord Mulligan would pay off the debts, but only on the condition that you would marry him, and with that marriage, our land would return to the family."

Sophie drew back, her chest rising sharply. "So my father used me as payment?" Her voice trembled with both shock and fury. Edwin's head bowed in shame as he nodded. Sophie turned away, pacing toward the window. Her reflection in the glass was pale as a ghost. For a long moment she stood in silence, steadying herself, before she exhaled a long, trembling breath.

Turning back, she faced them with resolve burning in her eyes. "Very well," she said at last. "I shall get to know the earl better and judge for myself what kind of man he truly is. I promise you this, Grandmama, Grandfather: I will not allow you to lose everything. If marrying him is the only way to preserve our land and estate, then so be it."

"No, Sophie, no!" Edwin cried, anguish in his voice. "We will not have you sacrifice yourself for our sake. We are old—we can endure whatever comes, even if it means leaving Grayside. But we will not see you condemned to a lifetime of unhappiness."

Augusta and Sophie were seated together in the parlor, the quiet rustle of pages the only sound as they read side by side. The fire crackled softly in the grate, casting a warm glow across the room—at least until the door opened and one of the maids stepped inside, her face taut with a mixture of nerves and urgency.

"Miss Everton," she said, dipping a quick curtsy, "the Earl of Adare is here to see you. Shall I show him in?"

Sophie's book slid closed in her lap as she glanced at her grandmother. A flicker of unease crossed her face, but Augusta's composure did not waver. With a steady nod meant to reassure her granddaughter, she addressed the maid.

"Please ask him to come in," Augusta said firmly. Then, softening her tone, she added, "and fetch my husband at once."

The maid curtsied again and hurried away.

Sophie bit her lip, a knot of dread tightening in her chest. She longed to ask her grandmother if she might be excused, but the words would not come. Before she could gather her courage, the door opened once more and the Earl of Adare entered the room.

He was tall, handsome, and dressed with meticulous care, the polish of London society clinging to him still. Both Sophie and her grandmother rose and curtsied.

"Lord Mulligan," Sophie greeted him with careful politeness, her voice steady despite the flutter in her chest. "What a surprise. What brings you here?"

He stepped closer with confident ease, taking her hand in his and bowing slightly, his manner practiced, almost rehearsed.

"Forgive me for intruding upon your privacy, Miss Everton," he began, his tone warm and unctuous, "but I was informed of the incident earlier and came at once to apologize in person for my servants' behavior. I had instructed them to invite you to my home to discuss our engagement and wedding plans. I never told them to coerce you. Rest assured, I shall deal with them accordingly." His green eyes fixed on her with an intensity that bordered on hunger. Though unsettled, Sophie returned a courteous smile.

"Thank you, Lord Mulligan," she replied. "I am glad you came to clarify the matter."

"Then," he said swiftly, seizing the moment, "will you do me the honor of joining me at my estate tomorrow?"

Before Sophie could reply, another voice cut firmly across the room. "I think, after what happened today, it would be best if Your Lordship were to visit Sophie here—at least until the official engagement has taken place."

Both Sophie and the earl turned sharply to see Edwin Everton standing in the doorway. His voice was calm, but the quiet authority behind it left little room for dispute. For a fleeting instant, something dark flickered in the earl's eyes—displeasure, perhaps, or surprise—but his expression smoothed almost at once. He inclined his head in a gracious nod.

"Certainly, sir," he replied evenly. "What time would be most convenient for you?"

"Perhaps in the afternoon," Edwin answered, his tone measured and firm.

"Until tomorrow then." The earl offered a shallow bow, which Augusta and Sophie returned, and within moments he had taken his leave.

The silence that followed pressed heavily upon the room, thick with unspoken fears and questions neither Augusta nor Sophie dared give voice to.

Sophie drew in a steadying breath. "Thank you, Grandfather. I truly didn't know how to respond. Surely Lord Mulligan must understand that it is highly improper for a single woman to visit a single man in his home unchaperoned. A man of his standing ought to know these rules as well as anyone." She shook her head, her expression troubled. "And beyond propriety—after what happened today, the thought of going there so soon, alone, filled me with unease."

Edwin's brow furrowed. "Yes, he should be fully aware. It

would be scandalous for you to present yourself at his estate without proper company. I daresay he put you in an impossible position." His gaze flicked toward Augusta, who nodded gravely before he continued.

"From this day forward, if your grandmother or I cannot accompany you, we shall at least send a servant or maid with you. A young lady of your age should always have a companion at hand. In truth, you ought to have your own lady's maid, but with our finances as they are, we can scarcely afford the few faithful servants we still employ."

Augusta shook her head, frustration slipping into her voice. "I still cannot understand why so many of our tenants left. We never raised their rents or taxed them more heavily. If anything, I thought we had been generous."

"Indeed we were," Edwin agreed, though his sigh betrayed his weariness. "But fortune has a cruel way of turning. Thankfully, Mr. McMahon spoke with me earlier. It seems several families from the town of Limerick are seeking to settle in the country. He asked if I might take on more tenants, and I assured him we could. Most will not arrive until spring, but within a fortnight we shall welcome two forest rangers and several livestock farmers onto our lands."

"That is wonderful news," Sophie and her grandmother exclaimed together, before exchanging a small, shared smile. Edwin nodded, some of the heaviness lifting from his expression.

"It is a blessing indeed. I must say, the steward of the Duke of Limerick works diligently and seems to know far more about our affairs than I expected."

Pleased for him, Sophie gave her grandfather a warm smile. "That is good to hear. I shall go to my room now and change for supper. You do remember, Grandmama, that His Grace and his companions are joining us this evening?"

Augusta's lips curved into a gentle smile. "I have not forgotten, my dear. Go on, I will see to the rest."

The moment Sophie was gone, Edwin stepped nearer to his wife, his voice low. "I did not like the feeling I got from the Earl of Adare. His manner was easy, even pleasant, but it felt rehearsed—as though he wore a mask. His apology did not ring true."

Augusta folded her hands together, worry shadowing her features. "I agree. He said all the right words, but there was little sincerity in them. Perhaps he is merely overworked, but I cannot shake the feeling that something else is at play. Best that we keep a watchful eye on him, and discover his true intentions."

The Evertons had scarcely informed their dinner guests of the unexpected honor—that the Duke of Limerick would join their table that evening—when the maid reappeared to announce His Grace and his two attendants.

Though the duke proved kind and quick with humor, putting even his steward at ease with genial remarks, Sophie could not help but feel a quiet sense of awe, even intimidation, in his presence. And judging by the subdued manner of her grandparents, she suspected they felt much the same.

Supper passed with lively conversation, yet beneath it all, a current of restraint lingered. When the meal concluded, Augusta extended an invitation for the duke and his men to return the following evening. They accepted warmly, their smiles genuine.

The ladies withdrew to the drawing room while the gentlemen lingered over port, as was customary. When they rejoined, the other guests soon excused themselves and departed for their own homes, but the duke and his companions chose to remain.

Augusta instructed a maid to bring in a tray of tea and biscuits. The flicker of lamplight softened the atmosphere, yet Sophie sensed that what was to be discussed next would carry far greater weight than polite pleasantries.

As soon as everyone had found a seat, the young duke cleared his throat, his expression grave.

"Rafferty, Seamus, and I have discussed the events of this afternoon and reached an agreement. Your granddaughter requires protection. If it pleases you, Rafferty will remain here and escort her wherever she chooses to go."

For a heartbeat, Sophie could only stare. Her breath caught, and she felt the steward's eyes upon her. To her dismay, her grandfather gave a firm nod of approval. Shocked, she shook her head quickly.

"Your Grace, that is very kind of you, but I cannot accept it. Mr. McMahon is your steward. His time should not be wasted looking after me."

Liam's gaze sharpened. "Miss Everton, he is not wasting his time. I have yet to meet the earl myself, but his servants—of that I am certain—cannot be trusted."

"Lord Mulligan himself called on me this afternoon," Sophie countered, her voice steady though her stomach churned. "He apologized for his servants' behavior. I am confident they will not trouble me again."

The duke exchanged a pointed glance with Rafferty before replying, his tone firm. "I fear you are mistaken. These men were not merely troublesome, they were about to abduct you. Had it not been for your dogs and our timely arrival, they would have carried you off. Kidnapping a young lady is a crime of the gravest kind, and I will not stand idly by until they succeed."

Sophie's eyes darted to her grandfather, silently pleading for his support. But his grave nod told her he agreed with the duke entirely. Heat rose in her chest, and she lifted her chin in defiance.

"Forgive me, but I do not need your protection," she said, her voice cutting with steel. "I am only the daughter of a physician, not a lady of consequence. I am not worthy of such safeguarding, Your Grace. I shall take care to bring a manservant with me whenever I walk. What will society think if I am seen trailed about by the steward of the duke? I have no standing to justify such attentions."

Lord Walsh's eyes widened, his expression one of surprise and disbelief. Slowly, he turned his gaze toward Edwin.

"She doesn't know?"

The old man's face clouded with discomfort. He shifted uneasily in his chair before shaking his head.

Sophie's heart gave a nervous thud. She glanced between them, her voice unsteady.

"Know what? What is it that you have not told me?"

Edwin sighed, rubbing a weary hand across his brow. "Sophie, please, do not be upset with us. Your father made us promise never to tell you."

Her pulse quickened. "Tell me what?"

Her grandfather hesitated, clearly ill at ease. "What do you know of your father's past, and of our ancestors?"

Sophie frowned, thinking hard. "Not much. Father never liked to speak of it. He avoided questions about genealogy, or what he did before he became a physician. All he ever said was that his great-grandfather surrendered a barony to pursue medicine, and that since then, our family had followed in that tradition. He was proud of our long line of physicians."

Edwin gave a small nod. "That much is true. My grandfather was the first to take up medicine, and every firstborn son has followed since."

Relief flickered across Sophie's face. "Then Father did not mislead me entirely. It is an honorable profession, one I believe even society respects." She smiled faintly at her grandfather, and he reached across to squeeze her hand.

"It is indeed honorable," Edwin said gravely, "but your father concealed other truths. My grandfather, and many before him, were noblemen. Neither he nor my father ever relinquished their titles." He paused, letting the words sink in. Then, his voice thickened with memory.

"My father was a baron, just like I am. When illness left him bedridden, it was my place to inherit the title. But it was then that Albert, your father, brought shame upon us. He took up with a young woman who was not his betrothed. She was poor, and she fell with child."

Sophie gasped, her hands tightening in her lap. The revelation struck like a blow. Edwin's face was grim.

"Her parents owned the inn where Albert stayed during his schooling. When the girl told him she carried his child, he denied it outright and refused to marry her." His voice faltered, heavy with shame. "It caused a scandal. Her parents, enraged, came to me with their story. I was mortified, and I promised them financial support once the child was born."

Sophie could scarcely breathe. The room had fallen into utter stillness, as though every soul within it held their breath, waiting to see what she would say.

After a long pause, Edwin continued, his voice low and heavy with memory. "When my father discovered what Albert had done, and that he refused to take responsibility for his actions, his disappointment was boundless. He blamed your grandmother and me, declaring that we had been too lenient—that Albert's poor manners and lack of restraint were the fruit of our indulgence. My father cut off every strand of financial support to us and our son and disowned Albert completely."

Sophie drew in a sharp breath. Her eyes stung, and she pressed a trembling hand to her lips. Near tears, she rose abruptly and crossed the room to the window, her skirts whispering across the floor. The chill of the glass steadied her, yet shame and confusion raged within her heart. To hear such things about her father, things she had never even imagined, felt like a wound laid bare.

At last she turned, twisting to face the others. Her gaze lingered briefly on the duke, whose eyes held only quiet sympathy, before returning to her grandfather. Her voice shook.

"I find it difficult to believe what I am hearing. Yet no one else seems even remotely surprised."

Edwin pressed his lips together, as though her pain cut him

deeply, but he continued, steady as stone.

"When Albert was cast out, he was left without means. He had always been selfish, accustomed to privilege, and believed himself entitled to do as he pleased. Stripped of that life, he grew bitter. In his resentment, he began weaving half-truths, convincing even you, Sophie, that our family had long since surrendered its title. That is not so. I remain Baron Everton." His eyes softened, regret shadowing his face. He gave his granddaughter a small, understanding nod before going on.

"Several months after his disgrace, Albert met your mother. They eloped in secret, without blessing or approval. Not long after, the young woman who had borne his illegitimate child gave birth to twin daughters. She did not survive the ordeal. Her parents were stricken with grief, and consumed by fury. They laid the blame entirely upon Albert, declaring that he had caused her death. Their anger ran so deep that they turned their backs on the infants, refusing to raise them." He sighed heavily before continuing.

"When your mother learned of Albert's past, she was devastated. Yet despite her hurt, she insisted on taking the infants as her own. She would not see innocent children punished for their father's sins. She raised them as your sisters, pouring all her love into them. But her loyalty cost her dearly."

Sophie felt the blood drain from her face. The room tilted slightly, and she gripped the back of a chair for balance. The duke and Rafferty both rose in alarm, but she lifted a trembling hand to ward them off. With slow, unsteady steps she returned to her seat and sank into it, her voice barely above a whisper.

"So... my sisters are only my half-sisters?"

Edwin inclined his head solemnly. "Yes. But, Sophie, there is more." He studied her face, as though weighing how much truth she could bear, then drew in a slow breath.

"When your mother's parents, the Fitzpatricks, learned of Albert's scandal and his refusal to marry the girl, they were incensed. They commanded your mother to leave him and return home at once. But she defied them, choosing instead to remain with the man she had wed. From that moment, all contact between them and your parents ceased. Albert was cast out a second time, disowned by both families. From then on, resentment poisoned his heart. He turned to drink, to gambling, to every vice that could numb his failures. We believed, in time, that we had persuaded him to abandon such destructive habits. We never realized how deeply his debts had mounted until it was far too late."

Sophie glanced at her grandmother and saw the pain etched across Augusta's face. The older woman's lips were pressed tightly together, her eyes shimmering with the ache of reliving old wounds. It struck Sophie then just how heavily these memories must still weigh upon them both. Her own voice trembled as she spoke.

"What I do not understand is why my mother's parents treated her so unkindly, so unforgivingly. They were only commoners, after all."

Augusta's head snapped up, shock flaring in her eyes. "Commoners? Is that what your father told you?"

Sophie nodded, confusion written plainly across her features.

"Do you know anything at all about them?" Augusta pressed, her tone gentler now, though still edged with disbelief.

Sophie shook her head slowly. "Hardly. Papa only said they were wealthy commoners who disapproved of him as a suitor. He told me my parents eloped, and that my mother was cast off and disowned for marrying beneath her family's expectations. Beyond that... he shared nothing. He forbade Mama from ever speaking of them."

Edwin and Augusta exchanged a heavy glance, then looked toward the duke before Edwin drew a deep breath and continued. His voice was steady, but weighted, as though he knew the truth would shake Sophie to her core.

"That is most unfortunate, for our son deceived you grievously. Your mother's family were not commoners, Sophie. Far from it. They live but a few hours' ride from here, on a great estate just outside Kilkenny. Their standing in life is vastly different from what your father led you to believe."

Sophie blinked at him, her confusion mounting. "Where do they live, then?"

"In Kilkenny Castle."

Her heart gave a startled leap. "A castle? Then—then my grandparents must have been servants there?"

Her grandfather shook his head, his eyes kind but unyielding. "No, child. The castle, the lands, and the villages around it all belong to the Fitzpatrick family."

"Fitzpatrick..." Sophie whispered, her mind racing. "That—that was Mama's maiden name."

"That is correct," Edwin said gravely. He exchanged another glance with Augusta before delivering the words that seemed to hang like thunder in the air. "Your grandparents are Lord Eamon Fitzpatrick, Duke of Kilkenny, and Princess Siobhan Fiona of the House of Windsor."

Sophie's knees buckled beneath her skirts, and she clutched the arm of her chair to steady herself. A dizzy spell swept through her, and for a dreadful moment she thought she might faint. She pressed a trembling hand to her chest, struggling for breath.

"That cannot be true," she stammered at last, her voice cracking. "I—I am Sophie Everton. Just Sophie Everton."

Edwin's eyes softened. "No, child. You were never 'just' Sophie Everton."

Her lips parted in a sharp gasp, her pulse thundering in her ears. "But that means—"

"Yes." Her grandfather nodded solemnly. "It means you are of noble blood. Royal blood."

The room seemed to tilt. Sophie forced herself to stand straighter, clinging desperately to composure though her whole world had shifted beneath her feet.

"Did my grandparents ever try to return to my parents' lives?" she asked at last, her voice low but urgent, as she sank back into her chair.

"They did," Edwin said gently. "After you were born, they reached out more than once. But Albert would not forgive. He refused any reconciliation, and he forbade your mother to seek them out."

Sophie swallowed hard. "And Mama? How did she feel?"

Augusta's eyes softened with sorrow. "She was not happy. She suffered greatly. But she stood by Albert—out of loyalty, and because she had chosen him of her own will. For better or worse, she would not abandon him."

Sophie fell silent, her thoughts a whirlwind. She sat very still, staring down at her folded hands as she tried to comprehend what she had just learned. Everything she thought she knew about herself, about her family, about her very place in the world—had been nothing more than a carefully woven lie.

4

The Calm Before the Snow

When the maid entered with the tea tray, the room fell into a hush. As the cups were set before them, His Grace cleared his throat, his expression steady.

"Can you understand now, Miss Everton, why I insist upon your having protection?"

Sophie stiffened, irritation rising in her chest. "And how is it that you know so much about this?" she asked, her voice edged with disbelief. "This is my family's private matter."

The young duke only smiled, a trace of amusement flickering across his handsome features.

"Because, Miss Everton, my grandparents and parents are close friends of your maternal grandparents. In fact..." He leaned back slightly, studying her reaction. "My father was once expected to marry your mother. It was one of the reasons your grandfather was so bitter when his only daughter chose to elope."

Sophie blinked, the revelation catching her breath. "I see," she murmured at last, her mind racing. After a pause, she lifted her gaze again. "Do you think they... would want to meet me?"

The duke's smile softened. "They cannot wait to meet you. I daresay you will see them at your engagement ball with Lord Mulligan."

Her gasp shattered the stillness. She turned at once to her grandfather, eyes wide with dread.

"Is that why Lord Mulligan wishes to marry me? Because of my grandparents?"

Edwin shook his head gravely. "No, child. To my knowledge, he does not know of your connection. Your father never spoke of it, and your grandparents honored his wish to keep it secret—because he did not want you to be an heir."

"But then why would they attend the ball?" Sophie pressed.

The duke gave a short scoff. "The Earl of Adare has been here but a short while, yet he spares no effort in surrounding himself with importance. He invites every prominent name within reach, hoping their presence will bolster his own stature. Ordinarily, His Grace would decline such invitations—he rarely attends the gatherings of men beneath his rank—but knowing you will be there, they have decided otherwise." He inclined his head toward her.

"I have little doubt Lord Mulligan will congratulate himself loudly when he receives their acceptance, believing himself elevated by their presence. He will not realize they come for you."

"They have not accepted yet?" Sophie asked, a frown furrowing her brow.

"No," the duke replied with a grin. "Lady Fitzpatrick, being of royal birth, rarely answers such requests until a day or two before an event. It is the way of her rank. Their lives are full, their duties many, and they seldom stoop to festivities beneath them."

"That sounds dreadfully prideful," Sophie remarked, rolling her eyes despite the pounding of her heart.

Lord Walsh chuckled softly. "It is how the ton works, Miss Everton. Besides, your grandfather, the Duke of Kilkenny, was once the Grand Duke of England before retiring here. When his father passed, he took up the duchy of Kilkenny. His rank and history are unlike any other in this part of Ireland."

Sophie sat in stunned silence, awe and disbelief battling within her. "And can I not go to them before the ball? To see them for myself?"

Edwin's face gentled, his voice kind but firm. "It is best to wait, Sophie. No one outside this room and the Walsh family knows the truth of your heritage. To call upon them without a proper invitation would raise questions we are not ready to answer. Let us keep the matter quiet for now." He gave her a reassuring look, and though Sophie's heart still ached with curiosity, she nodded.

Her father had done all he could to fill her heart with bitterness toward her mother's family, but her mother's voice echoed in memory: *Listen to your heart, child, and never let hatred govern your life.*

That same evening, Rafferty McMahon took up residence in the steward's cottage on the grounds of Grayside Manor. The dwelling had stood empty ever since the baron had been forced to dismiss his steward, unable to continue paying his wages.

Sophie protested heatedly, insisting such measures were unnecessary, but her grandparents stood firmly with the duke, declaring that her safety must come first.

His Grace returned again the following night, and the night after that. Sophie found herself increasingly vexed. How was it possible that one of the highest-ranking peers in the country had so much leisure to spend at their modest estate? Yet if her grandparents shared her doubts, they gave no sign of it. On the contrary, both Augusta and Edwin seemed to relish the company of the young duke and his loyal footman.

Rafferty, meanwhile, settled into the rhythm of the household with ease, his steady presence soon as natural as the ticking of the clock in the hallway. Though Sophie resisted at first, she could not deny a growing sense of safety in his watchful gaze—a protection she had never thought she needed, and now could not quite bring herself to refuse.

At the close of the evening, during his third visit to the Everton home, the young duke rose from his chair with a deliberate air. His expression, though warm, carried a formality that drew every eye in the room.

"Miss Everton," he said, inclining his head, "before I take my leave, I wish to extend an invitation to you and your grandparents. My sister, Lady Riona O'Sullivan, is married to the Marquess of Charleville in Cork, though one of their secondary estates lies not far from Adare. She has expressed a strong desire to make your acquaintance."

Sophie blinked in surprise. "Why would your sister wish to meet me?"

A small, knowing smile touched his lips. "I have spoken of you to her, and she is eager to meet you for herself. Would you do us the honor of joining them for a few days? I shall send a carriage in the morning."

Sophie glanced instinctively at her grandparents. Augusta and Edwin exchanged a look, then offered matching nods of approval. Still, Sophie could not quite fathom why Lady O'Sullivan, a marchioness no less, would be so interested in her.

Perhaps, she thought with a flicker of hope, it might be the beginning of a friendship. Loneliness had pressed heavily upon her since leaving England after her parents' deaths. The prospect of companionship with someone her own age stirred an unexpected warmth within her.

Her mind, however, remained clouded by the revelations of the past three days. So many truths about her family's history had been dragged into the light, leaving her unsettled. That the duke knew so much about her grandparents, more than she herself had ever been told, only deepened her discomfort. Embarrassment, even shame, rose within her like a tide, making it difficult to meet his steady dark hazel eyes.

She lowered her gaze to her lap, composing herself. Then, with effort, she lifted her chin and curved her lips into as genuine a smile as she could manage.

"It would be my honor to accept," she said softly, her voice steadier than she felt. A faint look of satisfaction flickered across his face before he bowed politely.

The following day, Sophie stepped into the gracious home of Lord Patrick O'Sullivan and Lady Riona. She had prepared herself for formality, for the polite reserve she so often encountered among society's upper echelons, but what she found instead left her disarmed.

"Lady Sophie Everton, it is such a pleasure to finally meet you," Lady O'Sullivan exclaimed with radiant warmth. A bright smile lit her lovely face as she extended both hands in greeting.

Sophie colored slightly and returned the smile, though she shook her head. "It is an honor to make your acquaintance, Lady O'Sullivan, but I fear you mistake me. I am not a lady. I hold no title."

Lady O'Sullivan's brows lifted in surprise. "But you are the granddaughter of Lord Fitzpatrick and Princess Siobhan, are you not?"

Sophie hesitated, then inclined her head. "That is true. Yet I have never met them, nor have I been formally introduced to society."

"Well, that simply will not do," Lady Sullivan declared with cheerful determination. "We shall change that as soon as possible." Her emerald eyes sparkled with sincerity as she added warmly, "We shall be great friends, I am certain of it. Please, do come in."

Sophie was astonished by the marchioness's kindness. Despite her noble rank, Lady O'Sullivan's manner was open and unaffected, her eagerness for companionship entirely genuine. To Sophie's delight, they appeared to be of a similar age, which only deepened her longing for the bond of true friendship.

As they moved further inside, Sophie observed the ease with which the marquess received her grandparents. His manner was courteous, but there was a particular tenderness in the way he glanced at his wife. When their eyes met, Sophie caught the unmistakable sparkle of affection that passed between them, and it warmed her heart.

Lady O'Sullivan, with her long dark hair braided neatly over one shoulder and her bright green eyes full of joy, was every bit as beautiful as she was gracious. It came as no surprise to Sophie that her husband so clearly adored her. Their love shone in every look, every gesture—so very different from the cold, businesslike arrangement that awaited Sophie in her own betrothal.

That evening, the Duke of Limerick joined them for supper. He greeted everyone with his usual easy charm, but almost at once he drew his sister aside and bent close to whisper something in her ear. The hushed tones, and the way Lady O'Sullivan nodded thoughtfully, left Sophie uneasy. Were they speaking of her? It felt impossible not to think so, yet propriety forbade her from asking.

When dinner was announced, Sophie found herself seated with the duke on her right and the marquess on her left. The arrangement left her little doubt: this must have been what the siblings had conspired over.

Though Sophie prided herself on her confidence and composure, she was far from at ease. Sitting so near the duke made her skin prickle with awareness. He seemed to know everything about her—her grandparents' struggles, her lineage, her looming betrothal—while she, by comparison, knew almost nothing of him beyond his title and reputation. The imbalance unsettled her.

And yet, beneath her unease, a more dangerous thought stirred. Did he see her as more than a guest beneath his brother-in-law's roof? He knew she was promised to another—her engagement to Lord Mulligan would be formally announced at the ball only days away. Surely he could not take a fancy to her. And yet... could he?

Sophie pushed such thoughts aside with a sharp inward scolding. Better to enjoy the evening than lose herself in impossible questions. And, to her surprise, enjoy it she did. The duke and the marquess possessed a natural wit that kept the table lively. Their stories and playful banter had everyone laughing until tears sprang to their eyes. Sophie herself could scarcely remember when she had laughed so much, or so freely.

The sound felt strange on her tongue, as though her voice had not known such joy in years. Her father had been a strict and serious man, with little patience for levity, and her mother—though tender—had always carried a quiet sorrow in her heart. That sorrow now seemed clearer to Sophie, perhaps born of burdens she was only just beginning to uncover. For one evening, however, she allowed herself to set aside grief and questions, basking in warmth and laughter.

As the night drew on, a storm gathered its strength outside. It began as a cold, steady rain that drummed against the windows, but soon the rhythm swelled into a roar. By the time dessert was finished, the rain had turned to snow—thick, heavy, and blinding as the wind howled around the manor. Fortunately, the animals had already been brought into barns and stables before the weather worsened, and inside, the company remained warm and secure.

By the time they retired, the storm was at its fiercest. The wind keened through the chimneys, rattling the panes with an almost human cry. In her chamber, Sophie found a cheerful fire burning in the grate, its flames licking upward and filling the room with a golden glow.

She changed into her nightgown, but despite the room's comfort, sleep would not come. Her mind churned restlessly—with thoughts of her parents, of her uncertain future, and of the duke, who unsettled her far too easily.

5

Compromised by a Duke

Seeking solitude, she gathered her shawl about her shoulders, slipped quietly from her chamber, and padded down the corridor. Near the staircase, a window alcove that had caught her eye earlier beckoned once more. Drawn by the storm, she stepped into its shadowed nook and pressed close to the glass.

The sight outside was both fearsome and beautiful. Snow blanketed the grounds, already piling into drifts that swallowed shrubs and fences. Fierce gusts tossed loose branches into the air like playthings. Ancient oaks groaned under the weight of the storm, their massive trunks bowing in protest. For one breathless moment Sophie thought one might be uprooted altogether.

She drew her shawl tighter around her shoulders, shivering—not from cold, but from the raw force of nature on display. There was something humbling in watching such power, something that made her feel very small. And yet, in the safety of the house, with its warm fire and strong walls, she also felt cocooned—caught between danger and comfort, fragility and shelter.

Other than the shrieking wind battering against the manor, the house lay in such profound silence that Sophie could hear the steady tick of a grandfather clock somewhere below. The sound was relentless, each beat a reminder of how swiftly her life had changed.

Her thoughts wandered back over the past year, a year that had stripped her of everything familiar. In a single afternoon, she had lost both parents, leaving her uprooted and sent across the sea to live with her grandparents in Ireland.

Her sisters were content in London, married and settled with families of their own, while Sophie's path had been altogether different. Instead of comfort and stability, she was left with secrets unraveling around her and the staggering discovery that her other grandparents—whom she had never even met—were not only alive, but of noble, even royal, blood.

The revelation unsettled her still. She, Sophie Everton, was expected to call dukes and princesses her kin. The notion seemed absurd. She had always believed herself the daughter of a physician, nothing more.

Yet darker questions loomed over everything—the unanswered mystery of her parents' deaths. Constables had investigated at the time, but no proof of foul play had ever been found. Still, suspicion lingered like a shadow that refused to lift.

Her brother-in-law, Constable Harrington—Gabriella's husband—remained convinced Albert Everton and his wife had been poisoned. The tea they drank that day had vanished with suspicious swiftness, the cups scrubbed clean before they could be examined. With no evidence, the case was closed, but unease clung to Sophie like a second skin.

Before leaving London, she had scoured her parents' chambers in desperation—searching for letters, diaries, even the smallest note that might give her answers. She knew her mother had kept a diary.

She had seen her bent over it often enough.

But it was gone. Its absence felt deliberate, as if someone had stolen or destroyed it to erase every trace of truth. And why would anyone do that, unless there was something damning to conceal? A shiver ran down Sophie's spine, and not from the draft seeping through the old windowpanes.

"Why are you still awake, Miss Everton? Is the storm keeping you up?"

The deep voice came from just behind her, and Sophie nearly leapt from her skin. Her heart slammed against her ribs as she whirled around, a cry caught in her throat. The Duke of Limerick stood there, his tall frame partly cloaked in shadow, his eyes softened with apology.

"Forgive me," he said, stepping closer with deliberate care. "I never meant to startle you."

Sophie pressed a hand to her chest, willing her breath to steady. "No, it is my fault, Your Grace. I was so lost in thought, I did not hear you approach." Turning back toward the window, she tried to calm her racing pulse. Out of the corner of her eye, she saw him draw up beside her, his gaze fixed on the storm.

The firelight from the corridor spilled across his broad shoulders, outlining the strength of his figure. Sophie forced her eyes away, scolding herself silently. It was not proper to notice such things, not when she was already promised to another. And yet, no matter how she reminded herself, her heart beat too quickly, her breath too shallowly, whenever he was near.

"Quite a storm out there," he remarked softly, the steady timbre of his voice nearly lost beneath the howl of the wind. "If it continues like this, we may find ourselves snowbound for some time."

Sophie nodded, her gaze still on the swirling white beyond the glass. The thought of being trapped should have unsettled her, yet with him standing so near, she could not tell if it was the storm—or the man beside her—that sent her pulse racing so wildly.

There was an awkward silence between them for several minutes, the storm's howl outside filling the void. Sophie cleared her throat softly.

"Your Grace, please allow me to thank you for introducing me to your dear sister. Lady O'Sullivan is truly lovable, and I am grateful to have found a friend again."

The duke turned his head toward her, his hazel eyes intent. His gaze lingered far too long, tracing the delicate line of her cheek before lowering—inevitably—to her lips. Heat rushed to Sophie's face, and she quickly cast her eyes downward, unable to endure the weight of his stare.

"There is no need to thank me," he murmured, his voice rich and low, carrying a warmth that seemed to vibrate through her. "My sister insisted on meeting you, and I was glad to oblige her wishes. Tell me, Miss Everton—was it difficult to leave London behind?"

The sudden change of subject jolted Sophie, and she stumbled over her words at first.

"It was hard," she admitted softly. "Hard to leave people I loved, the places I knew. But I have always loved Ireland. My heart feels at home here. When we visited my grandparents in years past, it was as though I belonged, even though they lived so far from town."

Before he could reply, a noise from behind the staircase startled them both. Sophie gasped as a dark shadow darted past. She stepped back in fright, catching her heel on a flower pot. She would have tumbled had it not been for the duke's strong arms closing around her.

Her breath stilled, her body pressed against his. The blood drained from her face until she saw, with immense relief, that it was only a cat bounding away into the corridor. But still she remained in his embrace, her pulse fluttering wildly.

His arm tightened protectively around her waist, steadying her, and she could feel the strength of him, the heat of his body seeping through her gown. His scent—warm spice and cedar—wrapped around her senses until she thought she might faint.

It was a perilous moment. She knew she should push him away. Yet when she lifted her eyes, she found his gaze locked on hers—an unguarded storm of yearning and unspoken desire. Her breath caught, her body stilled.

Then his lips found hers. It was no fleeting brush, but a heated, urgent kiss that stole her breath and set her world spinning. His hand cupped the back of her head, pulling her closer, deepening the kiss until Sophie melted into him, her heart hammering, and her knees weakening beneath her. For one intoxicating instant, she gave herself over to the warmth and fire of it, feeling as though nothing else in the world existed but his mouth against hers.

The realization crashed into her like a wave. Shock surged through her, and with trembling palms she pressed against his chest, pushing him back more forcefully than she intended. Anger, confusion, and longing warred inside her chest.

"Why would you do that?" she burst out, her voice trembling. "I am only days away from being formally engaged. Why would you, of all people, compromise me?"

The duke's lips curved into a faint, unrepentant smile, his hazel eyes glinting with mischief.

"Forgive me. I did not mean to anger you. I simply thought you wished for that kiss as much as I did."

Sophie's breath faltered—not from the kiss itself, but because he had read her so easily. His confidence unsettled her, and the half-smile tugging at his lips threatened to unravel her composure.

"I am disappointed in you, Your Grace," she said coldly, lifting her chin. "I would never have thought you a rogue."

He placed a hand to his chest in mock offense, his expression shifting into an exaggerated frown.

"One kiss, and already you censure me? My dear Miss Everton, that cuts deep."

She nearly laughed at the pitiful act but forced herself into composure. "A few days ago, you were a gentleman. Now this? Or are you only a gentleman when there are witnesses present?"

Instead of retreating, his eyes narrowed with determination. In one swift motion, he caught her hand and drew her against him once more. She gasped, her heartbeat leaping at his nearness.

"I do not believe you mean what you just said," he whispered, his voice low and fervent. "A true rake would not have stopped at one kiss." His gaze smoldered, his meaning unmistakable. Then, with visible restraint, he let her go.

Sophie clasped her hands at her waist, her eyes fixed on the floor, her face aflame.

"You must never kiss me again, Your Grace. There is no attachment between us, and I am promised to another."

He studied her in silence before asking, almost gently, "And if I proposed to you before your engagement was made official—would you accept me instead?"

Her head snapped up, disbelief blazing in her eyes. "That... that is no joking matter," she stammered.

"Who said I was joking?" he replied smoothly, not a flicker of doubt in his tone. Sophie stared at him, her heart thundering. At last she forced herself to answer, though her voice trembled.

"I would... politely decline your offer of marriage."

"Are you in love with Lord Mulligan?" he asked then, his tone softer now, his hazel eyes searching her face.

Her throat tightened. After a pause, she forced her voice into icy calm. "That is none of your concern, Your Grace." But the faltering note in her voice was answer enough.

Sophie's beauty was nothing short of breathtaking, and the young man found himself utterly captivated. When she spoke of Ireland, her whole face had come alive—her eyes shining, her lips curving with joy, her voice infused with warmth. In that moment, she had looked like a woman at peace, and he had been powerless not to admire her. He could have sworn he glimpsed something more than contentment in her gaze when he had held her earlier—a fleeting spark of desire that mirrored his own.

But she was not only beautiful, she was spirited. A playfulness lingered in her, a spark that danced in those brilliant blue eyes before talk of her engagement dimmed their light. That spark haunted him now.

Jealousy, sharp and unwelcome, gripped his chest. He had never envied another man before, yet now he resented the Earl of Adare with every fiber of his being. That cold, calculating man would have her as his bride, while he could only stand by, powerless. If only there were some way to prevent it...

"Sophie," he said at last, his voice low and earnest as he reached for her hand. Her delicate fingers trembled in his grasp, yet she did not pull away. "Do not marry a man you do not love. You would never know happiness."

Her lips parted, and for a heartbeat he thought she might confess to the same longing that consumed him. But her shoulders sagged, and her eyes, once bright, dulled with defeat.

"I'm afraid I don't have the luxury of choosing happiness or true love," she whispered, her voice breaking. "My father bound me to Lord Mulligan. If I refuse, my grandparents will lose everything. I cannot let that happen."

The sadness etched across her lovely face tore at his heart. He longed to gather her into his arms, to promise her another life—one filled with laughter, warmth, and freedom. His body ached to comfort her. But before he could move, a howl from the storm drew his eyes to the tall window beside them.

The trees outside bent dangerously in the wind. A sudden crack split the air, loud and sharp. With a gasp, Liam acted without thought. He swept Sophie into his arms, pressing her tightly against his chest to shield her. The crash came an instant later.

The window shattered with a deafening roar, shards of glass scattering like daggers across the room. A heavy tree limb burst through the frame, striking Sophie at the side of her head even as he tried to protect her. Her cry was brief before it was cut short, and then she went limp in his embrace.

"Sophie!" His voice broke loudly with panic as he cradled her tighter, shielding her from the icy gust that rushed through the gaping hole. Snow whirled into the chamber, already covering the floor at their feet.

6

Terms and Temper

Patrick and Riona came rushing up the staircase, their faces blanching at the sight of Sophie unconscious in the duke's arms. Behind them, Rafferty and several servants crowded the landing, wide-eyed with alarm.

"She is bleeding," Patrick said at once, his voice firm despite the fear in his eyes. He turned to his wife. "Riona!"

"Take her to her room," she urged swiftly, then looked to her brother. "Bring her—quickly."

The young man did not need to be told twice. He carried Sophie with desperate care, as though the slightest movement might harm her further. As they entered her chamber, Sophie's grandparents emerged from their own, their faces etched with terror. Augusta stifled a cry, while Edwin—his training as a physician overcoming his fear—stepped forward with authority.

"Lay her down here," he commanded. Once Sophie was settled upon the bed, he turned sharply to the others. "Out. All of you, out—except my wife and two maids. I need space to work."

Riona and her brother longed to protest, to remain at Sophie's side, but the steel in the old physician's eyes left no room for argument. With reluctance, they retreated, closing the door softly behind them.

In the corridor, the storm still raged. The shattered window had left the upper floor exposed to the howling wind and driving snow. Patrick turned swiftly, issuing orders with practiced calm.

"The storm isn't over. There are more trees close to the windows. Every shutter must be closed—from the inside only. It is far too dangerous to venture out." He fixed his gaze on the housekeeper and several maids. They nodded at once and hurried off.

"Cillian, Lorcan," Patrick continued, addressing the butler and steward, "fetch several room dividers from the maids' quarters and set them before the alcove. Use them to block the snow and wind. Nail blankets across the gaps if you must, and brace them with sturdy furniture. We cannot replace the glass until morning, but we must keep the cold at bay."

The men nodded firmly and disappeared down the corridor, already calling for tools.

Lord Walsh remained where he stood, his fists clenched at his sides, his heart hammering with the echo of Sophie's collapse. He could still feel the weight of her in his arms, the helpless slackness of her body as her head fell against his chest, and her warmth fading as unconsciousness stole over her. For the first time in years, he felt powerless. And he hated it.

Feeling ten times the rogue Sophie had accused him of being, he shoved his hands deep into his pockets and stepped up beside his sister. Riona turned to him at once, lifting her head to fix him with a frown.

"May I speak with you for a moment?" she asked. Her tone made it clear she was not requesting but commanding. Without protest, he followed her downstairs into the drawing room. Patrick joined them, his expression calm but expectant, as though he already knew this would not be a pleasant exchange.

Once the door closed, Riona wasted no time. "Why, pray, were you in the hallway outside Miss Everton's bedchamber?" Her voice was cool, her gaze unwavering, though the flicker of concern in her green eyes betrayed her agitation.

Her brother drew in a slow breath and let it out in a sigh. "I had not yet gone to my chamber. I saw Sophie walking toward the alcove window, and with the storm raging, I followed her."

Riona arched a brow. "Why would you do such a thing? You know how improper it is. What if a servant had seen you together—alone, at that hour?" She shook her head in disbelief. Patrick leaned one shoulder against the mantel, studying him steadily.

"I assume," he said carefully, "that you only spoke?"

The young man hesitated. "I kissed her."

Riona's breath caught, and she stepped closer. "You kissed her? You compromised her?" Her voice rose in disbelief. "Brother, I thought better of you. I truly did." She pressed a hand to her brow, then lowered it to glare at him. "You know full well she is promised to Lord Mulligan. The engagement will be made public in a matter of days. Why would you do something so reckless?"

"Because Mulligan is not fit to marry her!" he shot back, his composure cracking. "He is a scoundrel at best. You cannot possibly believe she would be safe or happy with him."

"You cannot possibly know otherwise," Riona retorted sharply. "There are whispers, yes—but whispers are not proof. I do not care for the man either, but hearsay that he mistreats his servants is hardly grounds for such outrageous behavior. You cannot go about stealing kisses from young women already promised to another, as though you had any right."

"It is not official yet," he snapped, pacing the room. His sudden intensity made the firelight leap across his face. "No one beyond this household knows Sophie is meant for the earl. Until the announcement, she is free."

"Goodness, Brother, do try to be reasonable." Riona's voice shook with indignation. "That is no excuse. You cannot justify recklessness by clinging to technicalities." She opened her mouth to scold him further, but Patrick raised a hand, stepping into the storm brewing between them.

"You do realize," he said evenly, "that if Lord Mulligan hears of this, he may demand satisfaction."

"I hope he does." Lord Walsh's voice was low but fierce. His jaw clenched, and his hazel eyes burned with defiance. "I would gladly meet him, gladly free Sophie from that cursed contract Albert Everton bound her to."

"You are a fool," Riona seethed, her eyes blazing. "What if you were killed in such a duel? You would be of no help to her then. You cannot protect Sophie from the grave, Brother!"

Her words struck like a slap, but he refused to back down. Her chest rose and fell rapidly, her fury threatening to spill into tears, until Patrick stepped firmly between them.

"That will do," the marquess said, his tone brooking no argument. "Both of you. Sit down and cool your tempers before you tear one another apart."

He turned to his wife first. "What your brother did was not wise, that much is clear. But there is a strong chance no one witnessed it, and he did keep her from grave harm when the window shattered. Had he not distracted her, Miss Everton might have been standing in the alcove when the tree struck."

Riona's hands trembled as she drew a deep breath. "She would have been safely abed if he had not distracted her," she countered bitterly.

"Enough, my dear," Patrick said firmly, taking her arm and steering her toward the door. "Go and rest. Let me speak with your brother alone."

Riona's lips pressed into a thin line. She cast her brother one last blazing look before sweeping from the room, her skirts rustling sharply with each step. The door shut behind her, and silence fell, broken only by the crackle of the low fire.

The two men lowered themselves into armchairs across from one another, the air heavy with unspoken words. Lord Walsh leaned forward, elbows on his knees, his hands clasped so tightly his knuckles whitened. Never had he felt more torn between desire and duty, and never more like the fool his sister had named him.

He wanted nothing more than to go upstairs and assure himself that Sophie was safe, but he knew the impropriety of such an action would only compromise her further. Restraining himself was agony. He gripped the arms of his chair, forcing his body to remain where it was.

Patrick leaned forward, resting his elbows on his knees, his hands clasped loosely together. His calm voice carried the weight of stern brotherly counsel.

"Brother, I understand the thrill of youth. A kiss can seem harmless enough, and Sophie Everton is indeed a striking young woman. But you must think beyond the moment. The last thing you want is to earn a reputation as a rake. Once society brands you so, it clings like a stain that cannot be washed away."

Lord Walsh's jaw tightened. "I care nothing for society's whispers. What I care about is her happiness. And I know—without a doubt—that she will be miserable if she marries the earl."

Patrick sighed, the note of experience heavy in his tone. "It is not for you to decide. You are nothing to Miss Everton in the eyes of her family or society. You are not her relation, not her betrothed. You have no right to interfere in the path laid before her."

"I would consider myself her friend," the young man countered, his voice low but resolute. Patrick's gaze hardened.

"Even as a friend, you hold no authority in this matter. Her father struck a bargain with Lord Mulligan, and Sophie is bound by that contract whether she wishes it or not. Even if you offered for her hand tomorrow, she could not accept you without bringing ruin upon herself and disgrace upon her grandparents. Do you truly wish to see her shunned by the very world she is about to enter?"

Lord Walsh surged to his feet, unable to contain his frustration. "Why would any father do such a thing to his daughter? What was Albert Everton thinking, or was he thinking at all? Sophie deserves more than to be bartered away like cattle." He raked a hand through his hair, pacing before the hearth.

"If I could convince her to elope, I would. I would do whatever it took to save her from that man. She doesn't deserve this. She doesn't deserve a loveless marriage."

Patrick's eyes followed him with quiet gravity. "You tread dangerous ground, Brother. Passion unchecked leads to ruin as swiftly as neglect. If you truly wish to help Sophie, you must find a wiser way than recklessness

Upstairs, Sophie stirred. Her grandfather bent over her, needle and thread in hand, his old physician's fingers steady despite his years. She winced at the sharp sting at her temple, squeezing her eyes shut against the pain.

"Almost done, child," Edwin murmured gently. "Breathe steady."

She clenched her jaw and obeyed, exhaling only when the final stitch was tied. A dull throb spread through her skull, and she managed a hoarse whisper.

"What happened?"

"You must have gone to the alcove to watch the storm," her grandfather explained, wiping the blood from her temple with careful precision. "The wind tore a tree from its roots. It crashed through the window, and a branch struck your head."

The memory rushed back. His Grace's lips on hers. The startling warmth of his embrace. The wild hammer of her pulse beneath his gaze, then the chaos of shattering glass. Her cheeks burned. She could not—would not—allow herself to dwell on it.

Why had he compromised her so recklessly? Why risk her reputation, even if no one had seen? She forced his handsome face from her thoughts, determined not to let him—or any man—confuse her. Sophie Everton would not be a plaything, not even for a duke. Surely she was nothing more than a passing distraction to Liam Walsh.

The storm left the estate battered and weary. Fallen branches littered the gardens, broken shutters dangled precariously, and even sections of the roof required repair. For days the servants labored tirelessly, hammering, patching, and sweeping while the wind still howled about the hills.

Confined to her bedchamber with a splitting headache and bouts of nausea, Sophie had little choice but to remain still. Her grandmother and Lady O'Sullivan visited often, their presence easing the long hours. Augusta's steady comfort and the marchioness's cheerful chatter softened the ache of loneliness, and slowly a warm companionship began to bloom between the two young women.

By the third day, Sophie was permitted to rise, though she still felt weak and dizzy. She resolved then to keep her distance from Liam Walsh. Whatever had passed between them, she would not give him, nor herself another opportunity to slip into impropriety.

Every time she heard his footsteps in the corridor, she quietly withdrew. Every time she sensed his gaze across a room, she turned away. Sophie Everton might be promised to another, but more than that, she was determined to keep her dignity intact.

Sophie and her grandparents returned to Grayside in the pale hush of afternoon, the sky the color of pewter and the fields still glittering with wind-battered frost. Rafferty helped her alight from the carriage, his manner unobtrusive yet attentive, and escorted her and her grandparents indoors.

They had scarcely shed their cloaks before Augusta reminded Sophie—apologetically—that they were expected elsewhere that evening. With a few murmured reassurances and a kiss to her brow, her grandparents departed once more, the front door closing behind them with a decisive thud that left the house feeling much too large.

Rafferty remained. At Sophie's request he took a discreet chair by the hearth in the drawing room, where a modest fire struggled valiantly against the chill. One of the maids, Elsie, stationed herself by the far wall for propriety's sake, hands folded neatly over her apron.

Sophie sank onto the settee, then rose again almost at once. Her head still throbbed in a dull, stubborn cadence, and the looming spectacle of her engagement—so close now as to feel inevitable—pressed against her ribs like a tightening corset.

She had told herself she had borne it all with composure these past days. But with the announcement only hours away, composure faltered. Fear pricked. Anger burned hotter. It was intolerable—this sense of being bartered, of being led toward a future she had not chosen.

She pressed her fingers to her temples, then began to pace a slow path between the window and the mantel, her skirts whispering over the carpet, the firelight catching glints of copper in her hair.

From his chair, Rafferty watched with quiet concern. "Miss Everton, is something amiss?" His voice was gentle, as if soothing a skittish mare. Sophie shook her head, but her mouth tightened—an answer and a refusal in one.

He seemed on the verge of trying again when the door opened and the housekeeper, Mrs. Doolan, stepped in with a careful curtsy.

"Miss Everton, the Earl of Adare wishes to see you."

Sophie stopped short. "What? At this hour?" Her gaze darted from the window to the housekeeper's face. "I cannot receive callers. My grandparents are from home."

"I informed his lordship," Mrs. Doolan replied, tone respectful but firm, "yet he refuses to depart without speaking to you. Shall I tell him you are not at liberty?"

Sophie hesitated, fists tightening in her skirts. The thought of meeting him alone turned her stomach, yet sending him away might unleash a worse temper.

"Not here," she said at last, her breath steadying. "Please show him into the parlor. I will join him directly."

"As you wish, miss." Mrs. Doolan dipped her head and withdrew.

Rafferty rose at once. "Shall I attend you?"

Sophie considered—only for a heartbeat. "No. It is best I speak to him privately." She softened the refusal with a faint, reassuring smile. "I shall leave the doors open. If you hear... anything untoward, pray come at once."

He inclined his head, understanding more than her words allowed. "Very good, miss."

Sophie drew a breath, smoothed her bodice with both palms, and slipped out by the side door. The corridor beyond was cool and dim. As she walked toward the parlor, she fixed her expression into something calm and impenetrable—armor fashioned from politeness. Whatever the earl intended, she would meet it on her feet.

7

She Will Not be Managed

When Sophie entered the parlor, she found the Earl of Adare lounging in an armchair as though it were his own drawing room. He sprang to his feet at once, executing a stiff bow. Sophie offered the requisite curtsy, though she kept her distance near the door. One glance at his darkened expression warned her to tread carefully.

"Lord Mulligan, what a surprise," she said with polite composure. "What brings you here this evening?"

His reply cracked like a whip. "Where were you?"

Her brows knit. "Pardon?"

"Where were you these last few days?" His green eyes flashed with suppressed fury. "I called on you repeatedly, and each time you were absent. The servants claimed ignorance, and I received no explanation."

Sophie almost laughed at the absurdity of his demand. Instead, she drew herself up with quiet dignity, though her pulse thudded hard in her throat.

"I was with my grandparents, My Lord. There was no cause for alarm." She tipped her chin higher, making it plain she would not be spoken to like a disobedient child. But he ignored the rebuke, stepping closer, his tone sharper.

"I expect to know where you are at all times. Leaving without informing me is unacceptable."

His cold, unyielding gaze fixed on her. Sophie's patience snapped.

"It is none of your concern where I was. I owe you no explanations. As I said, I was with my grandparents, and that is sufficient."

In two strides he loomed before her, his jaw rigid with anger. "Do not forget yourself, Miss Everton. In a matter of weeks, you will be my wife. That gives me every right to know your whereabouts. And I will not endure insolence from the woman who owes her father's freedom to me. Remember this well—had I not cleared his debts and spared him prison, you would not stand here so proudly defiant."

Sophie bit the inside of her cheek to keep from unleashing the retort burning on her tongue. She longed to tell him she would never be bought, yet she forced herself to remain silent. Mistaking her restraint for submission, he softened his voice with feigned gentleness.

"Now," he pressed, "where were you?"

Her anger simmered beneath her composure. "My grandparents and I spent the last three days at the estate of the Marquess of Charleville."

The earl blinked, clearly startled. He hesitated before regaining his voice. "Why?"

"Because they invited us."

"Invited you?" His disbelief was palpable. "They are far above your station. They have never extended an invitation to me."

Sophie's lips curved in a faint, sardonic smile. "They wished to make my acquaintance. Lady O'Sullivan showed me great kindness, and we have become dear friends."

His frown deepened, arrogance etched into every line of his face. Sophie's irritation flared hot.

"You must think very little of me indeed if you find it impossible that a lady might seek my company." She turned from him, gazing toward the tall windows to steady herself. There was a pause, then his tone shifted—quieter, calculated.

"I meant no offense. Forgive me, Miss Everton." He stepped forward and gently turned her to face him. "Please. Accept my apology."

His eyes seemed sincere enough that Sophie inclined her head in acknowledgment. But before she could withdraw, his hand shot up to cradle her cheek. Without so much as asking her leave, he bent and pressed his mouth to hers.

For a heartbeat Sophie froze, her blood turning to ice. Then fury surged. She shoved him back with sudden force.

"Lord Mulligan! We are not yet engaged."

"We are but hours away from our engagement," he countered with a smug grin, reaching for her again. Sophie held her ground, her blue eyes blazing.

"This is not proper," she said, her voice sharp with clarity. "I never gave you my consent. You will respect me, sir, or you will leave at once." Her tone left no room for argument. At last, the earl exhaled heavily, his lips curving into a thin, displeased line.

"Very well. I shall see you tomorrow evening. Would you like me to send a carriage for you?"

"That will not be necessary," Sophie answered coolly. "Lady O'Sullivan has already offered her conveyance."

The darkness in his eyes flickered once more, but he swallowed whatever bitter words rose to his tongue. With a curt bow, he turned and strode from the room, leaving Sophie trembling—but standing tall.

Sophie remained frozen where she stood until she was absolutely certain the earl had gone. Only then did the strength drain from her limbs. She collapsed into the nearest chair, seized a pillow with trembling hands, pressed it hard to her face, and released a muffled scream of sheer frustration and outrage.

The sound of footsteps made her jolt upright. Rafferty entered quietly, his steady gaze full of concern, though the faintest trace of amusement tugged at his mouth. Sophie's cheeks burned scarlet.

"Forgive me. That was not at all lady-like."

"I understand," Rafferty said evenly, though his jaw tightened. "Truth be told, I debated more than once whether to come in and throw him out myself."

Sophie exhaled, sagging against the chair. "He is an earl," she murmured, as though that excused the encounter.

"Still," Rafferty countered firmly, his hands curling into fists, "his behavior was that of a rake, not a gentleman. Title or not, no man should treat you in such a way."

"You're right, of course," Sophie admitted with a weary sigh. "I will not pretend I enjoyed his visit, or the way he scolded me as though I were a child, but..." She hesitated, guilt pricking at her. "I did leave without sending him a note. Perhaps I ought to have let him know where I was."

Rafferty's brows rose in disbelief. "Are you excusing his behavior because he did not know you were visiting the O'Sullivans? Miss Everton, that is no justification."

Sophie shook her head firmly. "No. His temper was what

unsettled me. It reminded me of my father."

The steward's expression softened. "Your father had a temper too?"

"Yes," she said quietly, her voice heavy with memory. "When anger overcame him, he treated my mother cruelly. She suffered far more than anyone knew, yet she never complained. I swore I would never endure the same."

Before Rafferty could reply, a maid entered to announce that her grandparents had returned. Rafferty inclined his head and hurried to assist them, leaving Sophie alone once more.

She turned to the window, pressing her palm to the cool glass as she struggled to quiet the storm within her. The earl's arrogance—his presumption that he had the right to command her, to chastise her—was outrageous. If he believed he could scold her like that as a husband, he was gravely mistaken. Her stomach turned at the memory of his kiss: stiff, possessive, utterly devoid of tenderness. Nothing about it stirred warmth in her. It left her cold.

But then, unbidden, the memory of another kiss rose in her mind. Liam Walsh's lips on hers, unexpected yet unforgettable. That kiss had stolen her breath, ignited her pulse, and filled her head with dizzying confusion. His scent, the warmth of his arms, the intensity of his hazel eyes—all lingered with dangerous clarity. Sophie shook herself, horrified that she was thinking of him at all.

"No," she whispered fiercely into the empty room. She could not allow herself such notions. There was no future with Liam Walsh. She was bound to Lord Mulligan, whether she wished it or not. Handsome dukes and romantic fancies were luxuries she could not afford. She would not let her heart betray her duty.

The next day, Sophie accompanied her grandparents and the O'Sullivans to the ball, arriving early. Her dark green gown shimmered in the candlelight, and both her grandmother and Lady O'Sullivan assured her she looked lovely. Even the earl himself offered effusive compliments, puffing with pride as he boasted of the 'honor' that the Duke of Kilkenny and Princess Siobhan had accepted his invitation.

Sophie's nerves tightened at the thought of meeting her maternal grandparents for the first time, and she could scarcely keep her hands from wringing. Lord Mulligan, however, seemed perfectly confident. He congratulated himself aloud, convinced that his supposed charm had reached the duke's ears at last. To him, their attendance was proof of his rising importance.

Sophie remained at his side, the earl scarcely allowing her to step away. He paraded her like a prized possession—always close, always within his grasp.

The next day, Sophie accompanied her grandparents and the O'Sullivans to the ball, arriving early. Her dark green gown shimmered in the candlelight, and both her grandmother and Lady O'Sullivan assured her she looked lovely. Even the earl himself offered effusive compliments, puffing with pride as he proclaimed the 'honor' of the Duke of Kilkenny and Princess Siobhan accepting his invitation.

Sophie's nerves, however, tightened like a noose at the thought of meeting her maternal grandparents for the first time. She could scarcely keep her hands from wringing in her lap. Lord Mulligan, by contrast, seemed perfectly at ease. He boasted that his charm must have reached the duke's ears at last, convinced their acceptance was a testament to his importance. He scarcely allowed Sophie to step away from his side, parading her like a prized possession—always within his reach, always displayed.

When Liam Walsh entered the ballroom with Rafferty at his heels, Sophie's heart stumbled. The young duke greeted Lord Mulligan with practiced politeness, yet when he bowed to her, his gesture was deeper, his dark hazel eyes lingering far too long. Her cheeks, already warm, bloomed crimson, and she dropped her gaze to hide it.

Then he smiled—warm, devastating—and Sophie's heart betrayed her, softening beneath the simple curve of his lips. Why must he look at her so intently, as though he could see straight through to the emotions she fought so desperately to conceal? Did he know how thoroughly he unsettled her, how his presence unraveled every defense she had so carefully built?

Of one thing Sophie was certain: Liam Walsh was no fool. He knew precisely what he was doing, and he was perfectly aware of the effect he had on her.

Lord Mulligan had received word that the Duke of Kilkenny would not arrive until the dinner hour. Relieved to enjoy the spotlight for himself, he greeted each guest with exaggerated charm, his hand resting possessively on Sophie's arm as though to display her as part of his triumph.

When the musicians struck up a lively waltz, even the elderly couples eagerly made their way to the floor. The earl turned to Sophie with a smile that did not quite reach his eyes.

"Come, my dear, let us open the dancing."

She allowed him to lead her forward, though her heart sank. From the first turn it was painfully clear that Lord Mulligan was no accomplished dancer. His steps were uneven, his timing uncertain, and he led her with such awkwardness that Sophie often had to guess which way he meant to move. Instead of floating across the polished floor, she felt jostled and tugged like a child at her first lesson.

Though she smiled politely, disappointment stirred in her chest. From his tight jaw she could see that he sensed it as well. At the close of the set, he excused himself stiffly, muttering something about being more a hunter than a dancer. Sophie curtsied and returned to her party, silently relieved the ordeal was over.

She had scarcely caught her breath before a familiar figure approached. Liam Walsh, the Duke of Limerick, bowed with impeccable grace and extended his arm.

"Miss Everton, may I have the honor of this next set?"

Her pulse leapt. Sophie's first instinct was to decline, knowing Lord Mulligan's temper would be ferocious. But refusing a duke's polite request before so many watchful eyes would itself be scandalous. Cornered, she inclined her head and placed her hand lightly upon his arm.

As another waltz began to echo through the ballroom, Liam led her onto the floor. From the very first step, Sophie knew she was lost. His hold was steady, his lead confident, and he guided her as though they had danced together a hundred times before. Their movements glided in perfect harmony—each turn seamless, each step a whisper of music come to life.

Her heart beat faster with every measure. She dared a glance upward and found his hazel eyes resting on her with a warmth that sent heat rushing into her cheeks. She quickly lowered her gaze, terrified that he might read the turmoil written across her face.

"You look beautiful tonight, Miss Everton," he murmured, his voice pitched low for her ears alone. Sophie forced a polite smile.

"Thank you, Your Grace."

The silence stretched between them until he spoke again, his tone darker now. "Rafferty told me of the incident with Lord Mulligan after you returned home. I must confess—I am disgusted."

Her chin lifted, her indignation flashing. "Rafferty had no right to share such information with you."

The duke's gaze deepened, and Sophie regretted her defiance almost at once. His face was so near, his eyes so intent, that the world around them seemed to fade away. Flustered, she broke the contact, her breath unsteady.

"Rafferty is my steward," Liam said firmly. "It is his duty to report such matters to me. More importantly, he is there for your protection. Please, Miss Everton, allow him to act when things go awry."

There was no arrogance in his tone, no desire to control—only genuine concern. Against her will, Sophie felt her heart soften.

"I thank you for your concern, Your Grace," she said quietly, "but I do not believe the earl wishes me harm."

"I beg you—be careful," he murmured, his gaze searching hers with an intensity that unsettled her. Her lips parted slightly before she found her voice.

"You don't trust him, do you?"

"No," he answered simply. "I don't."

The music drew to a close. With exquisite courtesy, Liam escorted her back to her party. He bowed over her hand before stepping away, but Sophie's eyes followed him as he crossed the room. An ache pierced her chest, sharp and unexpected.

She drew a steadying breath, fighting to master the swirl of emotions threatening to overwhelm her. She could not—must not—indulge such feelings. With her nerves frayed, she slipped away from her party, retrieved her shawl, and quietly slipped through a side door onto the terrace.

The cold night air rushed against Sophie's flushed cheeks—a blessed relief after the suffocating tumult of the ballroom. She drew her shawl tighter about her shoulders, willing her racing heart to steady. Why was she so annoyed, and yet so perilously drawn to Liam Walsh?

Her head snapped toward the terrace doors as they opened. A young woman stepped out with deliberate strides, skirts whispering in the chill. Sophie recognized her from earlier introductions.

Miss Mable Edington was undeniably beautiful, her dark curls framed a face made to melt hearts, but the gleam in her eyes was not one of warmth. It was sharp, cold, and brimming with malice.

"Miss Everton, may I speak with you?" Though worded politely, the clipped tone made it sound more like a command. Sophie forced calm into her voice.

"Perhaps we should return inside. It is bitterly cold, and we can speak in the warmth."

"No," Mable snapped. "We will talk here."

Sophie arched a brow, her blue eyes hardening. "As you wish.

What is it you want to speak about?"

"Your relationship with the duke."

Sophie blinked. "My relationship? We are acquainted, that is all."

"You would want me to believe that, wouldn't you?" Mable scoffed. "If that's true, then why did you have to kiss him?"

A chill sharper than the wind cut through Sophie. How could this woman know? She steadied her features, her voice even.

"I have no idea what you're talking about, Miss Edington."

"Stop lying. I know you've set your sights on him. Women like you always do—never satisfied, always reaching higher. The earl isn't enough for you, so you aim for a duke."

Outrage flared, heating Sophie's cheeks once more. "Watch your tone, Miss Edington. You accuse me of sins that are not mine. Perhaps you are speaking of yourself?"

"How dare you?"

"How dare I?" Sophie's eyes flashed. "You came out here to hurl insults at me, and I won't stand for it. I have done nothing wrong, nor have I ever claimed the duke as mine."

"You never will," Mable hissed. "Because he and I are courting. We are nearly engaged, which is why I know about the kiss."

Sophie felt the blood drain from her face but held herself tall. "Is that so? And did His Grace tell you that he kissed me, or did he leave that part out?"

Mable's lips curved in a smile devoid of warmth. "Don't worry, he behaved like a gentleman. He wasn't trying to ruin your reputation. But I know your type—you lured him in. Men are easily swayed when a woman plays the victim."

Sophie's chin lifted, her voice sharp as steel. "You must have quite a bit of practice at that yourself. How else would you know how easily men can be swayed?"

"You insufferable—" Mable snapped, her hands curling into fists. "Admit it. Admit that it's true."

Sophie's tone cooled into composure. "Why should I dignify your accusations? You wouldn't believe me no matter what I said."

"That's right," Mable sneered. "Because I already know the truth. The kiss meant nothing to him. I heard him myself, speaking to his footman. He said he only kissed you to see if he could get away with it."

The words struck like a blade. Sophie's heart twisted, but she refused to let Mable see her wounded. She fixed her with a withering stare.

"Then why waste your breath on me? If the duke is yours, go back inside and cling to him instead of harassing me. I have no interest in him. I made that perfectly clear to His Grace after the kiss."

"I am here to warn you," Mable snapped, her voice sharp as broken glass. "Stay away from him. And I want you to swear you will never set foot on his sister's estate again."

That gave Sophie pause. "What does his sister have to do with this?"

"How else will you avoid him completely? I have worked hard to build a relationship with his family, and you are in the way. Swear it, Miss Everton. Swear you will never visit Lady O'Sullivan again."

"I will not," Sophie said firmly. "My friendship with Lady O'Sullivan has nothing to do with you or His Grace."

Mable's eyes narrowed to slits. "Then heed my warning. If you don't do as I say, I will see to it that the Earl of Adare makes your life miserable."

8

Conditions Ignored

"You're out of your mind," Sophie said sharply. "I will not stand here listening to such nonsense. Continue your tantrum if you like, but your pitiful threats mean nothing to me." Without another glance, she swept past Mable, flung the terrace door wide, and returned to the ballroom—her head held high, even as her heart pounded.

As soon as the door fell shut behind her, Sophie drew in a sharp breath through her teeth. Her chest heaved with the effort of holding herself together. Part of her longed to collapse into the nearest chair and weep—for being treated so cruelly, for being accused and belittled, and for being so foolish as to let herself believe, even for a moment, that Liam Walsh might truly care for her.

She had always known there could never be a future between them. Still, the thought that he might have used her—that he had kissed her merely to toy with her feelings—cut deeper than she dared admit. Her throat ached, but she refused to cry. Anger surged instead, hot and unrelenting. She curled her fists until her nails pressed into her palms, fighting to master her emotions.

She nearly resolved to find her grandparents at once and beg them to take her home. But before she could take a step, Lord Walsh and Rafferty appeared, pushing quickly through the crowd toward her. The young duke's hazel eyes swept over her, concern etched in every line of his face. His voice was low and urgent when he reached her side.

"Are you all right? We've been searching everywhere for you. Did the earl—did he compromise you in any way?"

Sophie let out a sharp, incredulous laugh. "Why would you, of all people, ask me that?" Her blue eyes flashed as she met his gaze. "I believe you were the one who compromised me first."

Her words struck him like a blow. The Duke of Limerick froze, shock plain on his features, and even Rafferty looked stunned, his brow drawn tight. Neither man had time to reply before the earl's voice thundered across the ballroom.

"I have an announcement to make!" Lord Mulligan's booming tone silenced the musicians and stilled the dancers. A self-satisfied smile spread across his face as he raised a hand for attention. "Some of you may already have guessed, but it is my great honor to declare that Miss Sophie Everton and I are to be married. She has accepted my proposal, and we are formally engaged."

Polite applause rippled through the room, swelling into hearty clapping and murmurs of congratulation. The earl basked in it, bowing his head in mock humility, clearly reveling in the triumph. He did not so much as glance toward Sophie—as though the engagement were his alone to celebrate, not hers to share.

Sophie's stomach turned. She pressed her lips together and rolled her eyes, refusing him even the shadow of a smile. Then, out of the corner of her eye, she caught sight of Mable Edington. The young woman glided across the ballroom with deliberate grace, her gaze fixed on the earl. She reached his side with the air of a victor claiming spoils, her lips curved in a smile that might have charmed anyone else—but Sophie saw the malice simmering beneath.

Unease rippled through her. What game was Mable playing now? Sophie searched for some excuse to slip away, to escape this suffocating spectacle. But she was too late. Heavy footsteps pounded toward her. The earl.

His face was thunderous, his green eyes blazing with fury. Guests scattered as he stormed forward, his expression promising confrontation. And there, just behind him, stood Mable Edington, her vicious smile gleaming like a weapon.

"Your Grace!" Lord Mulligan roared, his voice reverberating through the ballroom before he even reached them. Conversation died instantly. All eyes turned to the enraged earl as he strode forward, fists clenched at his sides. "You and I need to talk."

Liam pivoted to meet him, his expression calm though his eyes narrowed in warning. "What is the matter, Mulligan?"

The earl's face darkened to crimson. "Trust me, you do not want to discuss this in front of my guests."

"I have nothing to hide," Liam replied evenly, his voice carrying the unmistakable weight of authority. "You may speak freely."

"How dare you compromise Miss Everton under the roof of your own sister?" Mulligan bellowed, his temper breaking entirely. "Do you think, because you are a duke, you may do as you please?"

Gasps rippled through the room. A wave of whispers and murmurs surged among the crowd like a rising tide—outrage, shock, speculation. Ladies fanned themselves furiously, men leaned to mutter to their neighbors. The scandal was already blooming.

Sophie's knees trembled beneath her gown. For a dreadful moment she thought she might faint. *So this is what Mable meant. This was the threat.* She forced herself forward and reached for the earl's arm, her voice low and urgent.

"My Lord, please—you are making a scene."

But Mulligan shook her off, his fury burning unchecked. His voice rose louder still, booming across the hall.

"You are just as guilty, Miss Everton. You push me away when I attempt to show you affection, yet you allow another man to compromise you? Do you think that proper conduct for a future countess?"

A chorus of horrified whispers filled the air. Sophie felt the heat of humiliation blaze across her cheeks. At the edge of the crowd, her grandparents stood stiff and stricken, their faces grave with shame. Riona and Patrick O'Sullivan hurried to her side, their expressions full of concern, as if to shield her from the verbal blows.

The earl pressed on, relentless. "I never expected such unseemliness of you—such graceless, unbecoming behavior! To shame me, your betrothed, in front of half the county and other esteemed guests—"

Sophie's breath caught painfully in her throat. Never in her life had she been so publicly humiliated, so exposed to judgmental stares and whispered condemnations. Her vision blurred with unshed tears, and she longed for the floor to open and swallow her whole.

Before Rafferty could tear the earl apart, he looked more than ready to, Liam stepped forward. His expression hardened as he clasped Sophie lightly by the arm and drew her protectively behind him.

"That is enough, Mulligan." His voice was steady, edged with steel. "Leave Miss Everton out of this. She has done nothing wrong. If there is blame, it is mine. I kissed her without her consent, without warning, catching her entirely by surprise. She scolded me for it and pushed me away. To accuse her of impropriety is outrageous. Her modesty and chastity are beyond question."

Gasps rippled again through the crowd. The earl's jaw clenched, his face dark with fury. "I demand satisfaction, My Lord," he ground out, his voice low but seething. "You kissed a woman already promised to another. You insulted my bride-to-be—and me."

Liam's eyes narrowed. His tone dropped to a near whisper, yet it carried like a blade through the charged air.

"Then let us go outside, Mulligan. I have been waiting for this opportunity."

The challenge sent a stir through the guests, but before either man could move, Patrick O'Sullivan stepped sharply between them.

"Enough," he commanded, his presence authoritative. "On what grounds, Mulligan, do you justify a duel with the Duke of Limerick?"

"On what grounds?" the earl thundered, his voice booming over the murmurs. "He compromised my betrothed! He has mocked my honor and her reputation."

Riona scoffed openly, folding her arms across her chest. "Forgive me, My Lord, but you are the one humiliating her. You are so blinded by your wounded pride that you've given no thought to how Miss Everton must feel. Instead of defending her, you drag her name through the mud in front of your guests. If anyone ought to be ashamed, it is you."

Her green eyes flashed like fire. With a disdainful sniff she added, "Women are supposed to be the fragile ones, yet I've never seen anything more delicate than a man's pride."

A ripple of muffled laughter moved through the guests, some failing to hide their smirks. Lord Mulligan's face flamed scarlet, his composure unraveling further under the sting of her words. Lady O'Sullivan's rebuke struck home.

The earl turned stiffly toward Sophie, his voice begrudging as he muttered, "Forgive me, Miss Everton."

Sophie met his gaze. His eyes held a flicker of contrition, though pride still simmered beneath. She inclined her head slightly. What good would it do to hold on to her anger now?

Patrick, still standing firmly between the rivals, pressed the matter. "Let us return to the facts. You accuse the duke of compromising Miss Everton, but was it public knowledge that you had claimed her as your future bride?"

The earl faltered, his lips tightening before he muttered, "No."

"Then it seems we are at an impasse," Patrick replied coolly. "By your own admission, you kissed the young lady against her will, just as His Grace did. That makes you both scoundrels in equal measure." His tone was dry, but his eyes twinkled as he cast Sophie a reassuring wink.

"The way I see it," Patrick continued, raising his voice for all to hear, "the only man with the right to demand satisfaction is Miss Everton's grandfather. After all, both of you dared to kiss his granddaughter without her consent—or his."

The room erupted in laughter. The tension, once thick as smoke, scattered into startled chuckles and relieved murmurs.

"I believe," Patrick added, his expression turning stern once more, "you both owe Miss Everton and her grandparents an apology."

Lord Mulligan, red-faced and fuming, strode stiffly toward the Evertons to mutter his forced contrition.

Before Liam could follow, Patrick laid a firm hand on his arm and drew him aside. "I warned you this would happen. You would be wise to leave after speaking with the Evertons. Do not linger."

Liam bristled. "And why should I slink away like a coward?"

"Because escalating this serves no one, least of all Miss Everton," Patrick said firmly.

"Just do as Patrick says," Riona interjected, her voice weary with exasperation. "He's right, and to be frank, your stubbornness is nearly as insufferable as Mulligan's temper." She rolled her eyes dramatically.

It was plain Sophie could see the duke wanted to argue further—his jaw was set, his shoulders rigid—but at last, he exhaled slowly, conceding with a curt nod.

"Well, if that is not an interesting welcome to a ball," a deep, commanding voice suddenly rang out, silencing the murmurs across the ballroom. Heads turned toward the great double doors that were wide open.

An elderly gentleman stood framed in the doorway, tall and imposing, his bearing unmistakably noble. Though his expression was stern, Sophie caught the faint twinkle of amusement in his eyes, a subtle spark that revealed more warmth than his rigid posture suggested.

Sophie's knees nearly buckled when a regal woman stepped gracefully across the threshold at his side. She knew her at once. The resemblance was undeniable—the same high cheekbones, the same delicate nose, and those eyes so reminiscent of her mother's, though touched now with age and wisdom. Sophie's breath caught in her throat. She had never met them before, but she knew instantly: her maternal grandparents had arrived.

The Earl of Adare, desperate to seize this moment for his own benefit, rushed forward to greet them with exaggerated enthusiasm.

"Your Graces!" he exclaimed, bowing low. Then, with a flourish of his hand, he waved Sophie forward, beckoning her into the spotlight.

Her heart thundered, but Sophie obeyed. She stepped forward slowly, and when she reached them, she sank into the deepest curtsy she had ever performed, her eyes lowered to the ground. She scarcely dared breathe.

The duke stepped toward her. Instead of waiting for her to rise, he reached out, took her hand firmly, and lifted her with surprising gentleness. His eyes never left her face, and Sophie felt her cheeks burn under the intensity of his gaze. She could see, in the way both he and the duchess looked at her, the yearning to embrace her at once, to claim her openly as their own. But for now, that tender intimacy had to wait—for no one here knew the truth of their connection.

"You made a wise decision, Lord Mulligan," the duke murmured, his voice low but edged with authority. "Only fools demand satisfaction over something so tedious, not to mention that it is illegal."

"Certainly, Your Grace, certainly. Welcome to my humble home." The earl bowed, words tumbling out in a stream of obsequious chatter. The duke endured it only a moment before stepping closer to Sophie and clearing his throat.

"And this is your fiancée?" His gaze flicked briefly to the earl before returning, pointedly, to Sophie. "I must say, you have an excellent eye for beauty, Lord Mulligan. Wouldn't you agree, Lady Fitzpatrick?"

The duchess inclined her head gracefully, her eyes softening as they lingered on Sophie's face.

"She is indeed a beautiful and charming young lady," she said with quiet conviction. Sophie curtsied once more, her voice timid but steady.

"Thank you, Your Graces."

The duke straightened, his tone brisk again as he addressed their host. "So, what is the plan for the evening?"

"Dinner will be served as soon as you wish, Your Grace," Lord Mulligan replied, a little too eagerly. This time, he checked himself, striving to appear less overbearing.

"Well then, let us dine. I confess I am famished." The duke smiled broadly. "Lord Mulligan, would you be so kind as to escort my wife to the table? I shall gladly follow with this young lady."

Delighted to be of use, the earl hurried to offer the duchess his arm, loudly declaring that dinner would now be served. With a gracious nod, she accepted, allowing him to lead her toward the dining room.

Left momentarily alone with Sophie, the duke turned to her fully. The smile that spread across his face melted her heart, for it was not the formal smile of a nobleman but the tender smile of a grandfather seeing his granddaughter for the first time.

"You look so much like your grandmother, and like your dear mother, Sophie," he said softly, his voice trembling with emotion. "My heart could burst with happiness to finally look upon you. Your grandmother feels the same, though she must contain herself until the truth can be spoken aloud or we are alone."

Sophie's eyes filled with tears she could scarcely contain. "I am delighted to meet you too, Your Grace."

"Now, let us settle one thing here and now," he said firmly, though affection warmed his tone. "In public, you may call me *Your Grace* until the truth of your lineage is revealed. But in private, I expect—no, I insist—you call me *Grandfather*." He gave her a playful wink. Sophie's lips curved into a trembling smile.

"I shall gladly oblige, Grandfather."

The duke's eyes glistened as he straightened. Then, offering his arm with solemn dignity, he said, "Miss Everton, will you do me the honor of accompanying me to dinner?"

"It would be my pleasure, Your Grace," she replied with a radiant smile.

"Ah, but please, child," he whispered conspiratorially as they began to walk. "Be kind to your old grandfather. A smile like that could melt even the iciest of hearts. If I were not careful, I might be tempted to pull you into my arms this very moment—and imagine the scandal that would cause, after an evening already full of them."

He was teasing, she knew, yet the warmth in his words set her cheeks aflame. And for the first time in days, her heart felt strangely light.

Dinner had been a strained affair. Though the table was laid with the finest delicacies and the company was distinguished, Lord Mulligan dominated the conversation from start to finish. He spoke loudly and incessantly—about his estate, his hunting dogs, his acquaintances in London—leaving little opportunity for the Fitzpatricks to exchange even a private word with their granddaughter.

Sophie endured it with polite smiles and carefully measured responses, though inside she longed for a moment of quiet in which to simply look upon her maternal grandparents, to hear their voices, to feel some sense of connection.

Her paternal grandparents, meanwhile, were seated with the O'Sullivans, and their kind presence was a small comfort. Yet even they could not dispel Sophie's unease. Lord Walsh had vanished entirely, and she could only assume he had departed at his sister's urging—a thought that pricked her heart more than she cared to admit.

At last, the final course was cleared, and Sophie exhaled softly in relief. Perhaps now the duke's suggestion of returning to the ballroom would allow the evening to shift into merrier spirits. But before anyone could rise, the earl pushed back his chair and stood, commanding attention. He cleared his throat and raised a hand. The room stilled. All eyes turned to him.

"Before we return to the ballroom," he began, his voice booming with self-importance, "I have one more announcement to make. Several of you asked me earlier when Miss Everton and I were to be married. Although we kept our attachment quiet, I have been planning this wedding for quite some time. It is my great pleasure to declare that our wedding shall take place on December the tenth."

A chorus of delighted gasps and murmured congratulations rippled through the room. Guests clapped politely, faces alight with curiosity and excitement. Sophie, however, felt as though the floor had dropped beneath her. Her gaze snapped to the earl, eyes wide with shock, but he only smiled smugly, basking in the admiration that poured his way.

When the applause died down and the earl turned to depart the table, Sophie reached out and seized his arm, her grip firm. Her voice was low but urgent.

"Lord Mulligan—that is only a fortnight away."

His grin widened, patronizing and playful. "I thought you would be delighted. I assumed you couldn't wait either." With a boldness that made her stomach churn, he attempted to slip his arm around her waist, but Sophie stiffened and held him off.

"That is not what I mean." Her words came quick and clipped. "My mother made it abundantly clear that this marriage could only take place if you abided by her conditions."

The smile slid from his face. His eyes, once gleaming with false charm, darkened with irritation.

"I don't know what you're talking about."

Sophie's chin lifted. "I believe you do. I heard my parents

talking about it and the stipulation of an exact wedding date was clearly mentioned. My mother insisted upon it."

He gave a sharp laugh, though there was no humor in it. "The letter I received stated only that they accepted my terms and proposal. You must have misunderstood."

Her composure broke for a moment, and anger flickered across her face. "I know what I heard. Do not dare dismiss it."

"Your mother is not here," he snapped, his voice lowering but growing more dangerous. "And I do not recall such foolish rules. It is decided, Miss Everton. The wedding will proceed as I have declared. I suggest you cease this melodrama and accept your good fortune. Now"—he extended his arm with a stiff smile—"let us return to the ballroom. Our guests await."

"No." The word cut through the air like a blade.

His brows shot up. "I beg your pardon?"

Sophie rose, her chair scraping softly against the floor. Her voice trembled only with conviction.

"I will not join you. This evening has been nothing but humiliating, and now you dare to feign ignorance of my mother's wishes? I am done." She turned sharply, skirts sweeping, intent on leaving. The earl's hand shot out, fingers clamping around her arm. His grip was tight, his face flushed with fury.

"You are not leaving. Our guests are waiting—"

She wrenched her arm free, her voice cold and cutting. "Your guests are waiting, not mine. Good night, My Lord." Without another word, Sophie swept from the room, her head held high. The silence she left in her wake was as deafening as the earl's announcement had been.

"Miss Everton, where are you going?" Lady O'Sullivan and the marquess had just stepped out of the ballroom when they noticed her hurrying toward the doors, her face pale with strain and her movements clipped with frustration.

"I'm leaving," Sophie replied, her voice tight and trembling with suppressed anger.

"Leaving?" Riona's brows drew together in shock. "Why?"

"Because I have had enough." Sophie's voice grew stronger with every word, spilling out like a flood she could no longer contain. "I don't wish to be controlled any longer, and I am tired of being attacked. I need time to think, and a walk in the cold air will do me good."

Riona stepped closer, lowering her voice as though confiding in a sister. "A walk? Sophie, it's dark outside, and wild animals are in the forest just waiting for such a chance. Let us take you home, please."

"No, you should stay." Sophie's reply was firm, though her eyes shimmered with unshed tears. Patrick moved beside his wife, his expression settling into the unyielding authority Sophie had seen in military men.

"We will not let you leave by yourself," he said flatly, leaving no room for argument. Before Sophie could protest again, another voice—deep, commanding, yet calm—cut through the tension from behind them.

"We will take her home," the man declared. They turned as one, and Sophie's heart nearly stopped when she recognized her maternal grandparents, the Duke and Duchess of Kilkenny. The duke stood tall and stern in the lantern glow, yet his gaze carried quiet protectiveness. At his side, the duchess leaned lightly on his arm, her face composed but softened with unmistakable concern.

"My wife is unwell," the duke continued smoothly, "and I believe Miss Everton's home is on our way. Please return to the ball and enjoy yourselves, we shall see that she arrives safely."

"As you wish, Your Grace." Patrick bowed at once, and Riona, wide-eyed, dropped into a curtsy. Sophie, overwhelmed, could only stare as her newfound grandparents stepped closer.

It seemed Lord and Lady Fitzpatrick had observed the entire exchange and, seizing their opportunity to have Sophie to themselves, acted at once.

"I already asked the butler to have our carriage waiting," the duke remarked with quiet satisfaction. The duchess's kind eyes swept over Sophie, noting her lack of outer garments.

"Do you not have a coat, child?"

"The servants took my coat," Sophie admitted, embarrassed. The Duke of Kilkenny beckoned a maid with a single gesture.

"We are taking this young lady home as she is unwell. Please fetch her coat at once."

The maid hurried away and returned moments later with Sophie's winter cloak draped neatly over her arm. Sophie accepted it with a grateful smile, murmuring her thanks.

"Shall we?" Lord Fitzpatrick offered, extending his hand. Sophie nodded, her chest tightening with emotion as her grandfather guided his wife carefully down the stairs toward the waiting carriage. Sophie followed close behind, her heart hammering with both relief and disbelief.

But just as she reached the open door of the chaise and bent to climb in, two strong hands closed firmly around her waist. With shocking swiftness, she was lifted off her feet and set directly inside the carriage as though she weighed nothing at all.

Sophie gasped, twisting around, her eyes flashing with outrage. "How dare you—" Her words broke off the instant she saw who it was.

Liam Walsh stood outside the carriage door, his hazel eyes glinting with mischief, a grin tugging at his lips.

"Oh, there is no need to thank me," he said lightly, his voice laced with infuriating charm. "It was my pleasure." He gave her a playful wink, executed a mocking bow, and vanished into the shadows at the side of the house—leaving Sophie flushed, indignant, and entirely speechless.

9

Arms of a Grandfather

Sophie slowly settled herself in the carriage, smoothing her skirts though her hands still trembled. Her face burned with indignation, the memory of Liam Walsh's audacity replaying over and over in her mind.

"I can't even..." she muttered under her breath, clutching at her bonnet strings as if they might steady her. "The audacity..."

Her grandparents, seated across from her, exchanged a glance. Amusement twinkled in their eyes, though they tried—unsuccessfully—to hide their smiles.

"What a charming gentleman," her grandmother remarked at last, her tone deliberately mild, though the corners of her mouth curved with mischief.

Sophie's head snapped up, scandalized. "Charming gentleman? Forgive me, Your Grace, but I couldn't disagree more. He is bold, cocky, and utterly impudent."

The duke leaned back in his seat with a grin that deepened the lines at the corners of his eyes.

"In other words," he said slyly, "you like him."

Sophie gasped, her hand flying to her chest. "What? No. I don't like him at all. He is—"

"...a handsome young man," her grandmother finished

smoothly, her smile widening with knowing warmth.

Sophie shot the older woman a frustrated glance, but despite her best effort, her lips betrayed her with the faintest of smiles. She lowered her eyes, her cheeks burning hotter still. As irritating and provoking as the Duke of Limerick was, even Sophie could not deny the truth—he was infuriatingly handsome.

The carriage rocked gently as silence settled between them, broken only by the rhythmic clatter of hooves on the frosted road. At last, Sophie looked up again, her voice softer.

"Does the driver know where I live?"

Her grandfather's expression warmed, and he shook his head. "Actually, child, we are not taking you home. You will stay with us for a few days."

Sophie's eyes widened. "But my grandparents will be worried sick."

"They already know," he assured her gently. "We've had this planned for some time."

"Oh." Her emotions shifted swiftly from surprise to wonder, a ripple of pleasure stealing through her heart.

"Will this be agreeable to you?" her grandmother asked, tilting her head with gentle concern.

Sophie nodded at once. "Yes, Grandmother."

The duke's smile deepened. "And in case you are concerned about your wardrobe," he added with a conspiratorial twinkle, "your grandmother has already thought of everything. She bought dresses and other attire you might need. In fact, she even had several gowns made."

Sophie blushed furiously. "You are so kind, but truly, you shouldn't have gone through all that trouble."

"It was no trouble," the duchess replied, her voice soft and steady. "Besides, we have been waiting for the day we might spoil you."

Sophie was in awe when she stepped out of the carriage. The castle her grandparents owned in the woods of Adare loomed before her, majestic and enchanting, rising from the heart of the forest like something conjured out of a fairytale. Moonlight shimmered off the snow-dusted turrets and stone walls.

For a moment, Sophie felt small, insignificant, and utterly underdressed. The massive doors opened before she could take it all in, and several servants lined the entryway, bowing and curtsying in welcome. Their quiet deference, combined with the grandeur of the house, nearly overwhelmed her.

She was led upstairs into a vast drawing room, its golden sconces casting warmth across polished wood and sumptuous tapestries. Sophie glanced around, still speechless. She had never seen such elegance, such beauty. For the moment at least, the unpleasantness of the ball was forgotten.

Servants soon brought in trays laden with tea and delicate pastries. Only after they had departed, leaving the three of them alone, did her grandfather step closer. His usually stern features softened, and he cleared his throat with uncharacteristic hesitation.

"Sophie," he said, his voice low and earnest, "now that we are finally alone and without witnesses... may I hold you in my arms?"

The young woman had not expected such a request. She looked up at the duke, her heart tightening as she saw eagerness in his eyes, tempered with patience. He would not move until she gave her consent.

"Certainly, Grandfather," she whispered. He took her hand,

strong yet gentle, and drew her firmly into his embrace. For the first time in her life, Sophie felt what it meant to be truly cherished by a fatherly figure. Her own father had never been affectionate, and her other grandfather rarely showed such tenderness.

But here, in her grandfather's arms, she felt wholly seen and entirely loved. Overcome, she burst into tears. The sobs shook her shoulders, yet the duke did not loosen his hold. He only drew her closer, pressing her head against his chest, letting her weep as long as she needed.

When at last her tears began to subside, he kissed the crown of her head and carefully transferred her into her grandmother's waiting arms. The duchess hugged her just as tightly, whispering soothing words as if she had been waiting years to comfort the girl.

And for the first time since the death of her parents, Sophie felt as though she truly belonged somewhere—somewhere beyond her Everton grandparents.

Seated before the warm glow of the fire, Sophie curled her hands together in her lap, the flickering light painting golden shadows across her grandparents' faces. Her grandfather cleared his throat, his expression solemn yet gentle.

"We want you to know, Sophie," he began, his deep voice steady but weighted with emotion, "that we loved you from the very moment we learned of your birth. Your grandmother and I have carried deep regret over choices we made concerning your parents, but please believe us when we say—we never stopped loving our daughter."

Sophie's heart squeezed painfully at the tenderness in his tone. She drew a slow breath, her voice quieter, tinged with hurt.

"Then why did you disown my mother? Did you hate my father that much?"

Eamon's sigh was heavy, burdened with years of unspoken sorrow. "We never hated Albert. But we had different hopes—different plans—for your mother's marriage. When I learned they had eloped, I was furious, blinded by pride. Your grandmother softened me, as she always does, but even so, I could not accept it."

"And then you discovered my father's illegitimate children," Sophie pressed, her voice trembling. "You wanted Mama to leave him?"

Her grandmother's hands folded neatly on her lap, but her eyes shone with compassion. "We hoped she would—so he might do right by the poor girl he had abandoned, left with no support and two daughters to raise. Yes, the scandal bruised our standing, but more than that, we were heartsick for her and her children. Albert refused, and when your mother chose to stand by him, we cut ties. It was not hatred, Sophie, it was desperation. But in our pride and anger, we made a grave mistake."

Her grandfather leaned forward, his gaze steady. "What we did not know then was that your parents later raised those two girls as their own, after their mother died. We did not learn the truth until after you were born."

Sophie's brows knit, confusion clouding her face. "How could you not know sooner?"

"Because your mother was deeply hurt," Eamon admitted, his voice thickening. "She would not speak to us for a long time. And she was right not to. Only after your birth did her heart soften enough to reach out." He glanced at his wife, then back at Sophie.

"She sent us a letter," her grandmother whispered, her lips

curving faintly with the memory. "She told us we were grandparents. As soon as we received her message, we tried to make amends. We longed to be part of your life. But Albert was unyielding. He would not forgive us. He forbade her to let us near you. He wanted you raised apart from us, without our influence."

Sophie's throat tightened. It was hard to imagine her mother defying her father, and yet...

"Did Mama still write to you?"

Her grandmother nodded, tears glistening. "Yes. Quietly, secretly. Not often, but enough. Once a year, at the very least, she found a way. Albert burned every letter we sent, but your mother... she always managed to slip us a note. Proof that she still wanted us in her life."

"And my father?" Sophie asked, her voice taut. "Did he never try to reach out?"

Her grandfather's jaw clenched. "Only once. He wrote to command us to stay out of your life. He made it clear you were not to inherit anything from us, that we were not to guide or influence you. His bitterness was unrelenting. Your mother stood by him, until near the end, when something changed."

Sophie's gaze sharpened, curiosity and dread mingling. "What changed?"

Eamon looked straight into her eyes. "I believe it was the matter of Lord Mulligan. Your mother wrote to us, asking us to look after you should anything happen to her and Albert. She wanted it to be your choice, Sophie—your decision—whether to let us into your life. That was her final request."

Sophie's breath caught. The blood drained from her face. "Do you mean... Mama expected to die?"

The duke exchanged a grave glance with his wife before

nodding. "Yes. We received several alarming letters from her shortly before her death. We sent an investigator, but..." He broke off, his voice low and hard. "He did not arrive in time."

The words struck Sophie like a physical blow. She rose to her feet and walked unsteadily to the window, her hands trembling against the frame. Her breath came unevenly as tears welled in her eyes. Why? Why would anyone have threatened her mother? What truth could she have carried that was so dangerous it might cost her life?

Her tears spilled freely now. She leaned her head against the cold glass, silently crying, until strong, steady arms folded around her. Her grandfather's embrace was firm, protective, and filled with love. He drew her back from the shadows of the window and held her close, as though he could shield her from every unanswered question.

Finally, Sophie raised her gaze to his face. "So there is a chance—" her voice cracked, but she forced herself on—"that someone murdered my parents? But why? They had nothing. My father had even been dismissed from the hospital because of his drinking. Why would anyone harm them?"

Eamon's eyes darkened with sorrow and resolve. "We do not yet know, my dear girl. But I promise you this—" he cupped her face in his large hands, his voice fierce with conviction—"I will not rest until the truth is uncovered. No matter how deep I must dig, no matter what enemies we must face, I will find the answers. For your mother. For your father. And for you."

When Sophie awoke the following morning, soft light streamed through the tall windows, painting the chamber in shades of gold and ivory. She stretched beneath the fine linen sheets and let her gaze wander.

The room was as grand as something out of a fairytale—high ceilings with carved beams, velvet draperies embroidered with silver threads, and a massive fireplace where embers still glowed faintly from the night before. For a fleeting moment, she truly felt like a princess.

Her father's parents had always provided her comfort and kindness, and their estate was handsome enough, but it could not compare to this castle. And to think—this was only the Fitzpatricks' country seat. She could hardly imagine what their principal castle in Kilkenny must look like.

A knock at the door startled her from her reverie. A young maid entered, bobbing a curtsy with a bright smile.

"Good morning, Miss Everton. Did you sleep well?"

"I did, thank you," Sophie replied, pushing herself up against the pillows. "Are—ehm—are His Grace and Princess Siobhan awake already?"

"Oh yes, for quite some time. Your grandfather rises early," the maid said cheerfully. Sophie blinked, her breath catching.

"My... grandfather?" Her cheeks warmed at the word. The young servant only smiled knowingly.

"Yes, Miss. I am to be your lady's maid whenever you are here. Their Graces told me who you are, but you needn't worry. Only the steward and I know, and neither of us will breathe a word. To the rest of the household, I'm to treat you simply as an honored guest."

Relief loosened the tension in Sophie's shoulders. "I see. And what is your name?"

"Oh, how careless of me." The maid dipped her head again. "I've not been in service long. My name is Fionn."

"Fionn?" Sophie repeated, brows lifting in surprise. "But isn't that usually a man's name?"

The maid's grin widened. "Yes, it is. My father was so certain I would be a boy that he declared my name would be Fionn—after the legendary hunter and warrior, Fionn mac Cumhaill. When I was born, the youngest of six daughters, he was so disappointed that he kept the name anyway. But he always said it suited me."

Sophie tilted her head, curiosity sparking. "Did he love you still?"

"Oh, yes. More than anything," Fionn replied with a tender smile. "Papa often told me the name was fitting, because I was the most curious of his children. I would follow him into the woods, asking endless questions, insisting I could hunt alongside him." Her laugh was light and fond, as though recalling cherished memories.

Sophie's heart warmed. She found herself already liking this spirited maid. "That is a charming story, Fionn."

The young woman beamed. "Thank you, Miss. Now, would you like me to help with your hair? Lady Fitzpatrick wishes to visit you as soon as you are ready, she is eager to show you the gowns she has prepared for you."

Sophie nodded, rising from the bed with renewed eagerness. She hurried to the dressing table, smoothing her nightgown as she sat. Fionn followed, gently brushing out Sophie's golden locks before twisting and pinning them into a simple, elegant style.

When Sophie looked at her reflection, she hardly recognized herself—her features seemed brighter, her smile freer, as though the heavy shadows of the previous evening had finally begun to lift.

A soft knock came at the door sometime later, just as Sophie had finished adjusting the sash of her dressing gown. She rose at once, smoothing her hair, and moved to greet her grandmother.

The Duchess of Kilkenny entered with a radiant smile, her elegance filling the chamber.

Fionn dipped into a graceful curtsy and stepped discreetly aside, allowing grandmother and granddaughter to embrace without interruption.

"You look lovely, Sophie. I trust you slept well?" the older woman asked, brushing a stray lock of hair from Sophie's face with grandmotherly affection.

"I did, Grandmother, thank you," Sophie replied warmly. "And you? Did you rest well?"

"Yes, very well indeed," her grandmother said, her eyes glowing with fondness. "But now it is time for us to find a gown for you. Fionn?"

At the duchess's nod, the young maid hurried to the wardrobe and opened its doors wide. Sophie's breath caught in her throat. Inside hung row upon row of gowns in the richest fabrics—silks in jewel tones, velvet trimmed in lace, soft muslins for daytime, and evening dresses embroidered with silver and gold thread. Slippers and gloves sat neatly arranged beneath them, while shawls and bonnets rested upon shelves.

"These are all mine?" Sophie whispered, eyes wide with disbelief. Her grandmother nodded, her smile broadening with satisfaction.

"Every one of them. They should fit you perfectly, and if by chance something does not, we will have it altered."

"I have never even seen gowns like these," Sophie breathed, her fingers brushing across the smooth satin of a pale blue dress.

10

It Is Miss Everton to You

"**I** know," the duchess replied softly, her gaze shadowed with sorrow. "That is why I may have gone a little overboard. I know your father kept you away from society and much of life's festivities. But you are our granddaughter, and your grandfather and I would like to see you presented properly. It is tradition, after all. When a young lady comes of age, her parents—or in this case, her grandparents—host a ball in her honor, presenting her to nobility and to potential suitors."

Sophie's smile faltered. "But I am already engaged."

"Yes, child, you are," her grandmother admitted with a sigh. She studied Sophie with perceptive eyes, then asked quietly, "But tell me truly, are you in love with the Earl of Adare?"

Sophie looked away, biting her lip. "I have to marry him, Grandmother. My father promised me to him, and he even signed a contract." She exhaled through her teeth, bitterness sharpening her tone. "As if I were some sort of cow to sell."

Her grandmother gave a startled laugh, and Fionn, unable to help herself, giggled behind her hand.

"You find that amusing?" Sophie asked, arching a brow.

"I find the comparison amusing, Miss Everton," Fionn said with a grin. "But no gentleman would mistake you for a cow. A true man would not pay for your affections, he would strive to earn them."

"Well said, Fionn," the duchess agreed warmly, drawing Sophie into another embrace. "Now, my darling, answer me plainly—do you love Lord Mulligan?"

"How could I?" Sophie's voice broke with honesty. "I hardly know him, and he has upset me more than once. It makes it... not easy to accept my fate."

The duchess's expression softened with compassion. "Then we will wait. There will be no debutante ball until you are certain. We will not have a man marry you for the wrong reasons."

Sophie shook her head, frustration mounting. "Grandmother, you make it sound as if I still have a choice, but I don't. I'm not of age yet, and my father made Lord Mulligan some sort of guardian over me until we are married. Not even Grandfather Everton has a say in the matter."

Her grandmother straightened, dignity radiating from her every word. "You forget, Sophie. Your grandfather and I are among the highest-ranking peers in Ireland. As the granddaughter of a duke, you will always have choices. Consequences, yes—but never the loss of your will, unless someone physically forces it from you."

Sophie's skepticism must have shown, for the duchess pressed on gently. "Your father was your guardian, yes, but you are your own person. Our daughter—your mother—proved that, though her choices pained us. We made mistakes with her, and she made mistakes of her own, but they were hers to make. And so it is with you. Never let anyone, be it your father or Lord Mulligan, convince you otherwise." She patted Sophie's hand with a reassuring smile.

"Men will try to make you believe you have no say, but that is a lie. And you, my dear, are no one's possession to barter."

Gratitude rose in Sophie's heart like a tide. Overcome, she threw her arms around her grandmother's neck. The duchess held her close, her embrace steady and full of love.

Together, they chose a soft lavender gown for the day. Once Sophie was dressed, her grandmother led her on a gentle tour of the castle. The marble halls gleamed, the grand staircases curved like rivers of stone, and everywhere Sophie looked, she found beauty.

But it was the library that made her stop short in wonder. Tall shelves stretched toward carved ceilings, filled with books bound in leather and gilt. A fire crackled in a marble hearth, filling the room with warmth.

Sophie's heart swelled with joy. This place, more than any ballroom or gown, made her feel at home. She was determined to return here as often as she could, though she suspected she might lose herself in its vastness and struggle to find her way back.

Eamon stood at the foot of the grand staircase, his sharp eyes softening as he watched his wife and granddaughter descend together. The sight filled him with pride. Sophie, with her fresh beauty and gentle grace, seemed to glow beneath the morning light streaming through the tall windows. He knew that once she was properly introduced to society, suitors would line up at their door, tripping over themselves for her favor.

"Look at this girl, darling," he exclaimed, his voice swelling with affection. "She will turn every head in the county. We'll have to keep the young footmen busy, or else they'll tumble over their own feet every time she enters a room."

Sophie's cheeks turned pink, and she shook her head, smiling despite her embarrassment. "I believe you are exaggerating, Your

Grace."

As if fate itself conspired to prove him right, two servants carrying trays of glasses hurried past them. Their eyes flickered—first toward Sophie, then back to their steps—but distraction won. They collided, and the sharp crash of shattering crystal echoed through the hall. Shards scattered across the marble tiles, followed by mortified apologies.

Eamon chuckled heartily, joined by Siobhan's warm laughter, while Sophie's blush deepened into a burning inferno. She wanted nothing more than to vanish into the floor. With a mischievous gleam in his eyes, her grandfather reached for her hand, offering a sheepish smile as he led her down the last few steps.

"Just as I thought," he teased. "You've already set chaos in motion. Now, to save the rest of my household from calamity, would you join me for a walk in the park?"

Still flustered, Sophie nodded silently, her gaze lowered to the floor. She pitied the poor servants who continued bowing and apologizing profusely, but the duke waved them off with good-natured reassurance.

A moment later, Fionn appeared with Sophie's winter coat, bonnet, and gloves neatly in hand. She winked at her mistress before darting away, leaving Sophie to hide a reluctant smile as she dressed for the cold.

The crisp winter air nipped at her cheeks as they stepped outside, but Sophie welcomed the chill. It cleared her head and cooled the heat that still lingered there. The park spread out before them, the grounds dusted with frost, bare branches glittering faintly in the pale light. Her grandfather offered his arm, and she slipped her hand through it with gratitude.

"There is something I must speak to you about," he began, his tone serious. "Your grandmother and I saw how distressed you were last night, how humiliated you felt by the events at the ball. I also had a long word with your father's parents, and what they said confirmed what I already suspected."

Sophie's throat tightened, but she forced a steady voice. "Last night was unfortunate," she admitted, eyes fixed on the gravel path beneath their feet. "But what did you suspect, Grandfather?"

"That nobody can force you to marry Lord Mulligan." His tone was firm, final. "I am well aware of the situation, Sophie, and though your father forbade us to take part in your life, I will not stand by and watch you sacrificed to a loveless match. If it is money the earl wants, I will gladly pay him myself to release you from the arrangement."

She stopped in her tracks, turning to face him, her eyes wide. His words struck her with both comfort and shock.

"That is a generous offer, Grandfather, and I am grateful—truly—but I could never accept."

"Why not?" he pressed gently, his brows knitting together.

"Because it isn't your debt to pay. I cannot have you bear the burden of my father's mistakes. It is not your fault, and you should not suffer for it."

Eamon's gaze softened, though his jaw set stubbornly. "And yet, it is not your debt either. The entire business is wrong from start to finish. Your father should never have dragged you into this. Allow me to put it right."

Sophie shook her head, determination flashing in her eyes. "Grandfather Everton would never accept your money unless there were a way to repay it. And even then, I doubt Lord Mulligan would agree. I recently learned that after my parents passed away, a family friend offered him a generous sum, and he refused. No, what he wants isn't money. He wants control. He wants to see the Everton family humiliated in every way possible." Her hands clenched at her sides as the realization hardened inside her.

A sigh escaped Eamon, followed by a rueful smile touched with regret. "You remind me so much of your mother just now—her fire, her stubbornness, her temper. You carry her spirit, dear girl."

Sophie's eyes shimmered, but she pressed on. "And how would we explain it if you did offer money? We can't reveal that I am your granddaughter—not yet, not before the wedding. Lord Mulligan is arrogant enough already. If he discovered I was tied to you, he would only gloat louder and tighten his grip. His pride does not need more fuel."

Eamon's expression darkened. He drew a deep breath and then spoke with grave sincerity.

"Promise me something, Sophie. If the day comes when you know—truly know—that you cannot go through with this marriage, that it will cost you your happiness, your dignity, or your freedom, you must end it. Do not let anyone bind you to a man who would make you miserable—not for land, not for estates, not for all the gold in Ireland. Your worth is greater than any bargain struck by men."

Emotion swelled in Sophie's chest, and she blinked back tears. Her voice trembled, but her resolve was firm.

"I promise, Grandfather."

Sophie escaped into the library after lunch, grateful to be away from the bustle of the household. Outside, snow had begun to fall in thick, drifting flakes, cloaking the grounds in white. At Fionn's direction, servants had built a glowing fire in the hearth, and the warmth mingled with the faint scent of leather and old parchment.

Fionn herself sat quietly in an armchair, content to watch her mistress drift from shelf to shelf, fingertips trailing over the spines, pausing now and then to read a few lines before setting the volume aside.

When the maid was called away to assist the housekeeper, Sophie crossed to the tall windows. Her breath caught as she watched the snow swirl and dance in the air. It was enchanting—each flake like a feather from heaven, turning the world into a living fairytale. She closed her eyes, inhaling deeply, letting the calm wash over her.

"What a pleasure to find you here, Miss Everton."

The familiar baritone made her whirl. Her pulse leapt as she saw him—Liam Walsh—leaning casually in the doorway, his lips curved in that insufferably confident grin.

"Good day, Your Grace," Sophie managed, though her voice trembled with both irritation and something perilously close to anticipation. "What are you doing here?"

"Your grandparents invited my family and me to dinner. Surely they told you?" His hazel eyes searched her face with unmistakable intent. Heat rushed to her cheeks. Of course they hadn't told her—deliberately, no doubt. She forced her chin up.

"No, they did not. Perhaps it slipped their minds. Now, if you will excuse me, I should join them downstairs." She swept past him, but in one swift movement he stepped into her path, close enough that she could feel the warmth radiating from him.

"Why the hurry?" he murmured. "I doubt they miss us yet. Stay a little longer."

"That would not be wise," she said firmly.

"You don't trust me?" His challenge was softened by the teasing glimmer in his eyes.

"As a matter of fact, I do not. The last time we were alone, you took advantage of the situation." She moved to sidestep him, but her foot caught on a pile of books. With a startled cry, she stumbled. In an instant, Liam caught her hands, pulling her firmly against his chest.

"That was a close call," he said, smiling down at her, his breath warm against her temple. Sophie's heart pounded wildly. She averted her gaze, struggling in vain to free herself, but his nearness muddled her resolve. His strong arms wrapped around her, steadying her—holding her far too close.

"Thank you...for catching me," she whispered, mortified by how unsteady her voice sounded. Before she could gather herself, his lips found hers—firm, heated, and far too sure. For one stunned second her body betrayed her, but then fury surged. She shoved him back, her cheeks aflame.

"How dare you?" she cried. "You compromised me once before and I was humiliated because of it, and now you dare again? I am engaged to be married!"

He looked utterly unrepentant. "Then I suppose I must go to your grandfather and confess what I have done, so that we might be married instead."

Her shock lasted only a heartbeat before indignation blazed. "Never! I will not marry you. You are a rake and should be ashamed." She spun toward the door, but once again his arms captured her, pulling her back.

"If I am a rake," he whispered wickedly, "then I may as well act like one." He cupped her face in his hands and kissed her again—harder this time, with a passion that stole her breath before she fought him off.

Tears of fury stung her eyes as she wrenched free. "Who do you think you are? Do you believe that because you are a duke you can do as you please? Am I nothing more than a game to you, a jest among your friends?"

Amusement flickered in his gaze, infuriating her further. "Why play with my feelings? Wasn't it enough to boast that you kissed me? Must you add to your sport by compromising me again and again?"

His grin faded at last, a frown darkening his features. But Sophie pressed on, her voice trembling with righteous anger.

"Why isn't one woman enough for you? Marry her—propose to her and leave me in peace. She has already attacked me once, humiliated me in public. I will not endure another scandal because of your reckless pride." She pushed against his chest, but his grip held fast. His hazel eyes had hardened, all levity gone.

"What are you talking about?"

"Don't feign ignorance." Yet even through her fury, Sophie glimpsed genuine bewilderment in his expression.

"I truly do not know what you mean," he said quietly. Her heart faltered for half a beat, but pride steeled her again.

"Do you take me for a fool? Then let me enlighten you. Miss Mable Edington cornered me at the ball. She claimed you and she are all but engaged, that you kissed me only to brag of it later. She threatened me, threatened to rouse Lord Mulligan's temper if I did not promise to stay away from you and your sister. And she kept her word. It is because of her that the earl publicly disgraced me."

Liam dropped his hold, his face pale with shock. "I swear to you, I have no idea who this Miss Edington is."

Sophie's laugh was bitter. "You expect me to believe that? Ridiculous." She swept toward the door, fury lending her speed.

"Sophie, please. I promise—"

She whirled, her glare icy. "It is Miss Everton to you, Your Grace." With that, she slammed the door behind her, leaving him alone among the firelight and the snowflakes drifting against the window.

Fionn entered her mistress's bedchamber not long after Sophie had returned from the library and found her pacing the room like a caged bird, her temper simmering just beneath the surface.

"Miss Everton, your grandparents' guests have arrived. Would you like me to help you get changed?"

Sophie didn't even turn around. Her voice was clipped, her back rigid. "I won't be going to dinner."

Fionn blinked. "Are you unwell?"

"I am well enough," Sophie replied, pressing her hands together in agitation, "but I am out of spirits and have no desire to be around people."

"Would you like to talk about it?"

Sophie shook her head, her pacing unbroken.

Fionn wrung her hands, clearly torn. "Do you wish me to fetch your grandmother so that you might confide in her?"

"No." Sophie stopped at the window, staring out into the fading light. After a long pause, she drew a breath and said more firmly, "I would like to speak to my grandfather. Please ask him to come to my room."

"Certainly." Fionn curtsied and slipped away at once.

11

A Will of her Own

She found her master in the parlor with his wife and their guests. The duke sat with a calm smile, listening politely to a tale being spun by Lord Lennon Walsh.

"Your Grace," Fionn interrupted with a respectful curtsy, "Miss Everton asked me to fetch you. She wishes to speak with you."

Lord Fitzpatrick's brows lifted slightly. "I suspected as much," he murmured, setting his glass aside. Rising to his feet, he turned to his guests with an apologetic smile. "It appears an urgent matter requires my attention. Please forgive me, I shall return shortly." He gave a conspiratorial wink to Fionn before striding from the room.

A minute later, his knock sounded firm against Sophie's door. "Come in," came her strained reply. Eamon entered to find his granddaughter standing at the window, her hands twisting together as if she could wring her frustration into submission.

"You wanted to see me?" His tone was gentle, though his eyes were watchful.

"Yes." She turned halfway toward him, her voice taut. "Why was I not informed that Lord Walsh would be joining us for dinner tonight?"

Eamon heard the sharp edge in her question and coughed into his hand to conceal a grin. "It isn't just him, Sophie. His parents, grandmother, sister, and brother-in-law are here as well."

"That doesn't answer my question."

"You seemed rather upset with the young man last night," Eamon explained mildly. "Your grandmother and I thought it best not to ruin your day with the knowledge. Surely you can endure his presence for a few hours?"

"No. I cannot."

"Why not?"

Sophie finally spun to face him, eyes blazing. "Because he is not a gentleman. He treats me with disrespect and behaves like a rake around me."

Eamon raised a brow. "Oh? And how so?"

Color rushed into her cheeks as she admitted, "His Grace found me in the library, and kissed me again. Not once, but twice."

Eamon drew himself up, feigning outrage though his eyes twinkled. "Atrocious! I shall speak to him at once and insist that he marry you."

"Marry him?" Sophie stamped her foot in indignation. "Never in a million years. I am already engaged, and yet he still compromises me. He should be publicly disgraced." She caught his look then, realizing he was teasing, and glared. "Grandfather, this is no joking matter."

"I know, child, forgive me," Eamon said, though his mouth twitched. "What would you have me do, then?"

"You should at least throw him out," Sophie declared. "But if I were you, I would give him a thorough scolding first."

Eamon chuckled under his breath, but the fire in her eyes warned him not to push further. He reached for her hand, drawing her nearer.

"Have you considered," he said softly, "that Lord Walsh may have taken a fancy to you? That perhaps he does not want you to marry Lord Mulligan?"

The suggestion robbed Sophie of words. She flushed crimson and looked away, but Eamon tipped her chin up with a finger until her gaze met his.

"I do not approve of his methods," the duke continued, "but I have known that boy all his life. He is no rake. He would never mistreat a lady without some cause. Everything he does is deliberate—well-thought-out, even if it appears otherwise."

"Then pray explain," Sophie retorted, "why Miss Edington attacked me yesterday. She claimed to be courting His Grace. That she was nearly engaged to him. She insisted he kissed me only to boast of it later."

Eamon's brows knit. "Miss Edington? Who is she?"

"You don't know her either?" Sophie's surprise was plain. She quickly recounted the confrontation at the ball.

The duke frowned. "Forgive me, my dear, but that doesn't sound right at all. If I had to guess, I would say she is a young woman trying to ensnare a wealthy husband. As I am not familiar with the local gentry, we know little of such names. But Lord Walsh and his steward should know who she is, if she indeed resides in or near Limerick."

"His Grace claimed not to know her either," Sophie admitted with a sigh.

"Then perhaps she has moved into the area only recently," Eamon mused, though Sophie's worried frown deepened. He pressed a kiss to her brow, his tone tender now. "Now, my dear girl, will you please join us for dinner?"

Sophie pouted but at last gave a reluctant nod.

"Good," he said with a wink, grinning at her discomfiture before leaving her to Fionn's capable hands to prepare her gown.

"So you are the infamous Miss Everton," Lord Lennon Walsh remarked with a genial smile. Sophie dropped into a graceful curtsy, though her brow furrowed in slight surprise. She had not expected to meet an elder Lord Walsh that evening—after all, Liam already bore the title of duke.

Only after a quiet inquiry to her grandfather did she learn the truth: the young duke had inherited his late uncle's duchy of Limerick, as that branch of the family had no male heir. Lord Lennon Walsh, Liam's father, was in fact the Marquess of Tipperary, whose lands bordered both Limerick and Kilkenny.

The elder lord's shrewd gaze swept over her, and then he turned to the Duke of Kilkenny with a satisfied nod.

"Your Grace, I must say—she is a very becoming and beautiful young lady."

"That she is," Eamon Fitzpatrick agreed without hesitation, pride softening his stern features.

Lord Lennon's eyes twinkled with mischief as he beckoned his son forward. "What is your opinion, Son?"

The young Duke of Limerick stepped up beside his father, his presence immediately commanding attention. His hazel eyes sought Sophie's, and when they found her, his lips curved into that heart-melting, infuriating smile that had unsettled her far too often.

"I must agree with you, Father," he said smoothly, his voice rich with warmth.

Sophie bit her lip, lowering her gaze quickly to keep her composure. Politeness demanded she smile, but inwardly she bristled at the ease with which he unnerved her.

Lady Saoirse Walsh joined them then, her manner gentle, and her eyes kind. She reached out to squeeze Sophie's hand with feminine warmth.

"What a shame that she is already engaged. A marriage between your granddaughter and our son would finally unite two of Ireland's most prominent families. Imagine the strength of such a bond."

A murmur of agreement rippled around the group, the suggestion treated almost as if it were self-evident. Heat rushed to Sophie's cheeks and crept down her neck. She felt cornered, their approving glances leaving her with nowhere to look.

Fortunately, Lady O'Sullivan stepped forward, her voice cutting through the moment like a blade. "Must you all make Miss Everton so uncomfortable? Leave her be. You are embarrassing her."

The room grew still for a heartbeat, and then Lady Walsh's expression softened with contrition.

"Forgive me, Miss Everton. I did not intend to make you uneasy."

"It's quite all right," Sophie murmured, forcing a small, shy smile. "I understand."

Before anyone else could press the subject, Riona deftly took Sophie's arm and drew her aside, leading her toward a quieter corner of the parlor. Sophie exhaled in relief, grateful for the young woman's rescue. The two conversed in hushed tones until the butler announced supper.

To Sophie's dismay, however, the reprieve did not last. At table, she found herself placed directly between the Duke of Limerick and his father. Liam's presence on her left was disconcerting enough. Every time she caught his gaze, her pulse quickened despite her best efforts to ignore him.

But Lord Lennon, on her right, proved just as forward, filling her ears with observations, questions, and pointed compliments. Sophie smiled and answered as politely as she could, but inwardly she longed for the quiet sanctuary of her chamber.

After the food had been served and the platters cleared away, the servants quietly withdrew, leaving only Fionn in the dining room. She stood discreetly against the far wall, ready to serve or summon help should it be required. The room felt smaller without the bustle of footmen, and the soft hum of conversation carried easily from one end of the table to the other.

It was Eamon Fitzpatrick who broke through the murmurs with a question directed at the young marchioness.

"Lady O'Sullivan, were you able to send that letter to the earl?"

Riona nodded, setting down her wineglass. "Yes, I was, Your Grace."

Sophie looked between them, her brows drawing together. "What letter?"

Her grandfather turned to her, his voice steady, almost casual. "I asked Lady O'Sullivan to write to Lord Mulligan in your name, explaining that you would be spending several days with relatives and would call on him again once you had returned."

Sophie's fork slipped against her plate with a soft clatter. "Why?"

"Because," Eamon explained gently, "considering Lord Mulligan's temper and his need to feel in control, it seemed wise to assure him of your whereabouts. We wanted him to believe you were merely taking time away to recover your composure after the ball."

Although Sophie knew the reasoning was sound, irritation prickled beneath her skin. "Why could I not have written the letter myself?"

Her grandmother gave her a sympathetic smile. "Because we wished you to rest, my dear. You have been distressed enough. Was that so wrong of us?"

Sophie exhaled slowly, caught between gratitude and exasperation. "No... it was considerate. But still, I ought to have written it. What if the earl discovers that Lady O'Sullivan pretended to be me?"

Before anyone could respond, Liam Walsh's voice cut across the table like a blade.

"Why don't we call off the engagement altogether and send Lord Mulligan where he belongs?"

The boldness of the declaration stunned the room into silence. All eyes turned toward him.

"Son," Lady Saoirse Walsh said sharply, shaking her head at him, her expression both reproachful and weary. But Liam leaned forward, his jaw set, his gaze fixed on Sophie.

"Do we not all agree he doesn't deserve her? That man has neither the temperament nor the decency to be her husband."

Sophie froze, her hands tightening in her lap. She stared down at her plate, heat flooding her cheeks, before she forced herself to straighten.

Her voice trembled with anger as she replied, "This is not your decision to make, Your Grace. Nor is it a matter to be discussed at this table."

"I agree," Riona interjected, glaring daggers at her brother. "I have told you before, brother, that we cannot know for certain that Lord Mulligan is truly a bad man. Yes, he has a quick temper and can be overbearing, but I could say the same of others present." Her eyes lingered meaningfully on the young duke. But her brother refused to relent.

"He is not a good man, Riona, and you know it. Sophie will be miserable if she marries him. Is that what any of you want for her?"

That was too much. Sophie's temper, long restrained, finally broke. She pushed back her chair and rose to her feet, her voice carrying with raw emotion.

"Will you stop speaking as though I am not in the room? I am not a child to be passed about or a prize to be quarreled over. My future is my own, and if this engagement is to end, it will be by my choice—or Lord Mulligan's. No one else's. Least of all yours, Your Grace." Her eyes blazed as she met Liam's gaze, and he flinched ever so slightly.

"I didn't mean it like that, Sophie," he tried to say, his tone softening, but the damage was done. Her fury sharpened her words.

"It is still Miss Everton to you, Your Grace." With that, she turned sharply, skirts swishing, and strode out of the room before anyone could stop her. Fionn hurried after her, with Lady O'Sullivan and her grandmother close behind, leaving an uncomfortable silence in their wake.

12

Under the Duke's Protection

"Well done, Son," the elder Lord Walsh muttered at last, shaking his head in disapproval.

"I don't want her to get hurt. Is that so wrong?" the young man demanded, his voice taut with frustration.

"No, it isn't," Eamon Fitzpatrick admitted gravely. "But we must tread carefully with her. She is proud, independent, and—" he sighed, his expression softening with memory, "—I fear she has inherited her mother's temper. You'll remember that, Lord Walsh," he added, turning to the marquess, "from when you courted my daughter."

"Oh yes," Lennon Walsh replied with a knowing smile. "I remember it well."

Sophie returned to her father's parents a few days later and, with careful wording, sent Lord Mulligan a letter informing him of her return. The earl wasted no time. That very afternoon, he called upon her.

She had just come in from a brisk walk in the garden, her cheeks rosy from the cold, when a maid announced him. Lord Mulligan entered with his usual air of self-importance. His gaze lingered on her flushed face, and he gave a low bow before taking her hand.

"How radiant you look, Miss Everton," he said, pressing his lips to her fingers. "The country air has done you good."

Sophie forced a polite smile. "Lord Mulligan, how kind of you to call."

"I am delighted to find you so well. It seems your absence has restored your spirits."

"Yes," she admitted evenly. "It was much needed."

He shifted, clearing his throat. "I must beg your pardon for my behavior at the ball. I know I angered you and left you distressed. That was never my intention. I even attempted to call upon Lord Fitzpatrick several times, wishing to apologize to him as well, but he refused to see me. I hope I did not offend him beyond repair."

At the mention of her grandfather's name, Sophie's heart lurched, though she kept her expression calm.

"It must have been embarrassing for him to witness such ungentlemanlike behavior," she replied with quiet firmness. "Perhaps you might write him a letter. That would be more proper than forcing your way into his study."

Mulligan frowned, unsettled, and then nodded slowly. "An excellent suggestion. I shall do so."

Once seated, Sophie folded her hands in her lap and studied him carefully. This was her chance.

"There is something I must ask you, Lord Mulligan. Who is Miss Mable Edington? She approached me at the ball—threatened me, in fact—and claimed to be intimately connected with you. Yet no one else seems to know who she is."

For the first time that afternoon, his composure faltered. His jaw tightened, and a flicker of irritation flashed in his eyes. Sophie's stomach knotted at once.

"Miss Edington?" he said after a pause. "Ah, you must mean Miss Mable Mulligan. She is my cousin. She came into the district not long after I did."

"Your cousin?" Sophie tilted her head, searching his face. "Does she live with you?"

His eyes narrowed ever so slightly. "No. She resides with a distant relative."

"Then why introduce herself as Edington?"

"She was married once," he answered curtly. "Her husband has since passed. Seeking a new beginning, she left England and came here."

Sophie softened her voice. "I am sorry to hear of her loss."

"Yes, well..." He rose abruptly, brushing away her sympathy. "She has not been the same since." Without lingering, he added, "Forgive me, but I must return home. Would you do me the honor of joining me for tea tomorrow? We must finalize our wedding plans. The day is nearly upon us." His eyes gleamed with satisfaction. "Only a week remains."

Before Sophie could gather her reply, Augusta Everton stood as well. She had been in the room as a chaperone, her presence a shield.

"I do not believe that is wise," her grandmother said firmly. "We have no female servant available to accompany her, and she should not be left alone with you."

Mulligan inclined his head, his smile tight. "Then I shall ensure my housekeeper and a maid remain present the entire time. Would that be agreeable, Lady Everton?"

Augusta hesitated but finally gave a measured nod. Sophie offered the earl a polite smile, though unease twisted in her chest.

"Very well, My Lord. I would be delighted to join you."

"Wonderful. I will send a carriage. Until tomorrow, then." He bowed deeply before striding out.

As the door closed behind him, Sophie released a breath she hadn't realized she was holding. She moved to the window where her grandmother already stood.

"Grandmama," she whispered, "do you think he was telling the truth about Miss Mulligan?"

The older woman's eyes remained fixed on the distant carriage wheels rolling away. "I do not think so, child. There was something in his manner I did not trust. He is hiding something, of that I am certain. The question is... what?"

The following day, Rafferty was ready. Having returned with Sophie from her maternal grandparents' estate, he refused to leave her vulnerable. When Lord Mulligan's carriage arrived to collect her, Rafferty mounted his horse and followed at a discreet distance. Neither he nor Sophie wanted the earl to suspect she was under the duke's protection, but both knew her safety depended on it.

Sophie was shown into the drawing room and left alone for scarcely a moment before the study door opened and Kenneth Mulligan appeared. He greeted her with exaggerated enthusiasm, his smile too wide, and his eyes slightly unfocused. Sophie's heart sank. Even from across the room, she caught the faint, unmistakable scent of alcohol clinging to him. Her whole body tensed, instincts on high alert.

"Where are your housekeeper and maid?" she asked, forcing her voice calm.

"They will join us shortly," he said with a dismissive wave of his hand. "Will you excuse me a moment? I must finish an overdue and rather important correspondence. It shan't take long. A servant will bring tea directly."

Sophie inclined her head, though unease crawled down her spine. Mulligan disappeared back into his study, leaving the door only partially closed. Silence settled again, broken only by the faint scratch of his quill.

Unable to sit still, Sophie drifted toward the open door and leaned against the frame. What she saw made her stomach twist. He sat hunched at his desk, scribbling furiously, a half-empty bottle of Brandy glinting in the firelight beside him, an overturned glass abandoned nearby.

She swallowed hard, her pulse quickening. Memories of her father's drunken rages crashed over her—his shouting, his cruelty to the servants, the way he had belittled her mother. Though Albert Everton had never raised his hand to his wife or daughter, Sophie knew too well how alcohol poisoned men, stripping them of honor and restraint. She clenched her fists. She would not take chances with Kenneth Mulligan.

While she debated whether to retreat and summon Rafferty, a sharp knock rattled the second door of the study.

At Mulligan's impatient bark of "Come in," a young maid entered, her hands trembling as she carried a tray of tea and biscuits. She set the tray on the edge of the desk and began to pour. The earl didn't so much as glance at her until the second cup was nearly full. Then, with startling suddenness, he lurched to his feet, his chair toppling against the wall with a crash.

"What do you think you're doing?" he thundered, his voice thick with drink. "I told you to take the tea to the drawing room, not in here!"

The maid flinched, stumbling backward, and stammered an apology. Mulligan's face contorted with rage. With a violent sweep of his arm, he sent the entire tray crashing to the floor, shattering china and splashing tea across the carpet.

"Forgive me, My Lord," the maid whispered, trembling. "I misunderstood, I—please..."

He advanced in two strides and struck her with the back of his hand, the blow so forceful she crumpled against the doorframe with a cry. Tears welled in her eyes as she whimpered, clutching the side of her face.

Sophie's horror flared into fire. Before he could raise his hand again, she shoved the door wide and rushed between them. Wrapping her arms protectively around the trembling maid, she turned on Mulligan with blazing eyes.

"How dare you?" she cried, her voice ringing clear and sharp. "What has this poor girl done to deserve such cruelty?"

"She made a mistake," Mulligan sneered, his lip curling. "And I do not allow mistakes."

"You do not allow them?" Sophie's voice shook with fury. "Everyone makes mistakes, My Lord, even you. To strike her for something so trivial is vile beyond measure."

He scoffed, waving off her reproach as though she were no more than a buzzing fly. "Go," he barked at the maid, ignoring

Sophie entirely. "Fetch what is needed to clean this mess. And if you dawdle or fail again, I will use the strap next time instead of my hand."

The girl's hands trembled as she scrambled toward the drawing room. Sophie darted after her, catching her arm before she could flee down the hall.

"Has he done this before?" she whispered urgently. The maid's wide, terrified eyes said everything, but at last she gave the smallest nod. The sound of Mulligan's boots echoed from the study as he followed, and the girl's breath hitched with panic. Sophie pulled her close, her voice low and fierce.

"Listen to me. Go to your room, gather your belongings, and leave this house. Outside, by the carriage, you will find a man—Mr. McMahon. He is here for me. Tell him I sent you, and he will protect you."

The girl's lips parted in fear. "But Lord Mulligan—"

"I will take care of him," Sophie interrupted firmly, though her heart thundered. "Go. Now."

With one last terrified glance, the maid nodded and hurried away. Sophie remained where she was, steeling herself, bracing for the earl's wrath as his heavy footsteps drew nearer.

Sophie turned the instant Lord Mulligan strode toward her. His grin was twisted, mocking, and it made her stomach churn.

"Don't trouble yourself over the girl," he said with chilling nonchalance. "She is only a servant. I have done far worse to those beneath me."

Revulsion surged through Sophie. She moved quickly, putting the settee between them like a barrier.

"I would not boast of such cruelty, My Lord. Servants deserve dignity and respect no less than you or I."

"Not in my house." His grin widened as though her defiance amused him. He reached across the settee and seized her chin, pulling her face close until she wrenched herself free. Her voice trembled with disgust as she straightened her spine.

"I shall leave now. You are drunk, and I will not stay another moment in your company." She swept past the settee, determined to reach the door, but before she could grasp the handle he was already there. Leaning against the doorframe, he barred her way, one arm sliding around her waist and dragging her back against him. His grip was suffocating, his breath hot against her temple.

"Let me go," she demanded, pushing against his chest with both hands. "Your behavior today is disgraceful."

He ignored her words entirely. Instead he clasped her tighter, burying his face in her hair, inhaling her as though she already belonged to him. Panic clawed at Sophie's chest. She struck him with her fists, her fear fueling her strength, but he only laughed—a cruel, hollow sound that froze her blood.

"If you don't release me this instant, I will scream for help," she warned, her voice sharp despite the terror coursing through her.

"No one will come to you, sweet Sophie," he murmured darkly, his grin curling back into place. "This is my house. My servants obey only me. You are mine, and in just a few days the world will know it. Why wait when I can have you now?" He shoved her backward into the room. The door slammed shut with a violent crack.

Sophie stumbled, desperate for escape, but he advanced relentlessly. When she tried to cry out, he crushed his mouth to hers, trapping her in a bruising kiss, his hands forcing her against him. Horror surged through her—every nerve screaming, every instinct demanding flight.

She shoved, clawed, and struck, but he held fast, driving her back until she collided with the settee. Then, at the very moment despair threatened to overwhelm her, he was ripped away.

Rafferty had burst into the room like a storm unleashed. His face was carved in fury, his entire frame trembling with contained violence. In one swift motion he seized the earl by the throat and slammed him against the wall.

"What in the devil's name—" Mulligan rasped, clawing at Rafferty's iron grip. "Who are you, and what are you doing in my house?"

"I am the duke's steward," Rafferty growled, his voice low and lethal. "And I am here to protect Miss Everton." His eyes burned with such wrath that Sophie, trembling by the settee, almost pitied the man in his grasp.

"The duke has no right—" Mulligan managed to roar, his face reddening. "It is not his place to protect my fiancée."

Rafferty's laugh was cold and contemptuous. "Someone must protect her. If you will not honor her as a gentleman should, then His Grace has every right to intervene." He leaned closer, his voice dropping to a deadly promise. "You are no man. You are a coward and a scoundrel. Mark my words, Mulligan: if ever again you dare raise your hand against this young lady, or any lady, I will not hesitate to end you.

Rafferty shoved the earl away with such force that the man stumbled against the wall, sputtering in outrage. Without waiting for another word, he slipped an arm firmly around Sophie's trembling frame and guided her out of the house. The icy air outside struck her like a cleansing wave, though her heart still raced with terror.

He had wisely sent the carriage away earlier with the rescued maid, ensuring her safety before stepping foot inside Mulligan's house. That meant no conveyance waited for them now—only his horse, tethered nearby. As soon as they reached it, Rafferty glanced down at Sophie. The moment their eyes met, the fragile strength she had been holding onto crumbled.

Her body shook violently. Tears spilled down her cheeks as she collapsed against him. Without hesitation, Rafferty pulled her into his strong arms, holding her close to his chest.

"Shhh," he whispered roughly, his voice unsteady with fury and concern. His hand stroked her back, trying to soothe her trembling. She clung to him, her sobs muffled against the wool of his coat, but for the first time since leaving her grandparents' estate that morning, Sophie felt safe. Protected.

Rafferty's jaw tightened as he glanced back at the manor. His whole body trembled with the urge to return, to finish what he had started with Mulligan, to make the man pay for daring to touch Sophie. But her soft, broken plea stopped him.

"Please—don't. Just... take me home."

Her words, fragile though they were, carried more power than any order. He swallowed hard, forcing down his rage. She needed his strength, not his vengeance. He lifted her into the saddle, swung up behind her, and held her steady as they rode through the falling snow toward the Everton estate.

13

A Bargain with Chains

When at last they arrived, Sophie nearly fled from his arms, hurrying into the house and straight to her bedchamber. She needed solitude, a place where she could fall apart without anyone watching. She shut the door behind her, pressed her back to it, and then collapsed onto her bed. Bursts of sobs shook her as she buried her face in the pillows.

One thing was certain: she could not—would not—marry Kenneth Mulligan. No promise to her father, no signed agreement, no estate or title was worth the degradation of belonging to such a man. But the thought of what that decision might cost her grandparents, and their estate, sent a fresh wave of despair crashing through her heart.

Meanwhile, Rafferty wasted no time. He penned urgent notes and sent trusted messengers to the Duke of Kilkenny and to the Marquess of Charleville. Then he spoke quietly but firmly to Baron and Baroness Everton, recounting every detail of what had transpired. The baron and his wife listened in shocked silence, disbelief etched into their faces, until at last Baroness Augusta covered her mouth with trembling fingers.

"I never imagined... not like this," she whispered. They agreed Sophie must not be pressed to speak of the matter unless she chose to. The trauma was too raw, and the decision about her future had to come from her alone.

Two hours later, Sophie descended the staircase, pale but composed, her eyes faintly red from weeping. Baroness Augusta greeted her in the drawing room with a sweet, loving smile that nearly undid her all over again. Her grandfather was absent, and she assumed he remained in his study.

She drifted to the tall window, staring out at the snowfall. The world outside looked so calm, so pure, as if nothing terrible had ever happened. Yet inside her chest, her heart was a storm.

The door opened behind her, and more than one voice reached her ears. Sophie turned, startled. Both her grandfathers entered the room—Baron Everton and the Duke of Kilkenny—followed by the Duke of Limerick, Rafferty, and Lord and Lady O'Sullivan. The sight of so many familiar faces, all gathered on her account, stole her breath.

"What is everyone doing here?" she asked, her voice unsteady. Lady O'Sullivan hurried to her side and wrapped her in a warm embrace.

"Oh, Sophie..."

Sophie's eyes immediately shot to Rafferty, narrowing into a glare sharp enough to cut.

"Forgive me, Miss Everton," he said, his tone firm but apologetic. "Those who care for you had a right to know."

Her heart twisted. She gently disentangled herself from Riona's arms and managed a practiced smile that fooled no one.

"I am sorry Mr. McMahon has troubled you all for nothing," she said quietly, her voice as brittle as glass. "I am perfectly fine. Truly. There is no need for concern."

With every pair of eyes fixed upon her, their sympathy pressing close, Sophie turned back to the window. The snow beyond was easier to face than the love and worry surrounding her.

The Duke of Kilkenny cleared his throat. His commanding voice cut through the heavy silence.

"May I have a word alone with my granddaughter?"

No one argued. One by one the others filed out, their faces full of concern and reluctant understanding. The door clicked shut, and the room fell quiet except for the soft crackle of the fire.

Sophie did not move. She stood stiffly by the window, her back to him, hands clenched in the folds of her gown. She heard his footsteps approach, steady and unhurried.

"Grandfather, there is no need to speak to me alone," she said quickly, her tone too bright, too brittle. "I am splendid." The lie sounded hollow even to her own ears. "In fact, I feel like taking a turn through the garden, if you will excuse me." She tried to slip past him, desperate to escape his searching gaze, but he stopped her with a gentle firmness, one strong hand guiding her back.

She kept her head bowed, fighting the tremor in her lips, but he would not let her hide. With infinite care he lifted her chin until her tear-filled eyes met his. At that single touch of kindness Sophie's composure shattered. Hot tears spilled down her cheeks as a sob tore from her, and before she could falter his arms were around her—strong and unyielding—pulling her against his chest.

No words were needed. He simply held her, steady as stone,

while she wept. Her tears dampened his coat. Her slender frame trembled in his embrace, yet he only tightened his hold, smoothing her hair with the knowing gentleness of a father soothing a frightened child.

At last, when the storm of emotion began to subside, he loosened his grip, though his arm remained steady at her back.

"Listen to me, Sophie," he said at last, his voice low but firm, full of authority and affection. "What you feel is not weakness, it is the wound left by betrayal and fear. Lord Mulligan overstepped every boundary of honor. There is no excuse for what he tried to do. I had intended to hold back, to let matters play out without my interference, but after this I cannot and will not stand by. You cannot marry that man. I will not allow it."

Her breath caught. "I know."

"You deserve happiness, child. You deserve safety, respect, and love — not a life of dread. With him you would know only fear, and that I cannot permit." He cupped her cheek, his thumb brushing away the last traces of her tears.

Sophie swallowed. Her voice trembled. "It is already decided, Grandfather. I ended it."

His brows lifted. "What do you mean?"

"There is no need for letters from you, or for escorts to face him. I have written to him myself. The letter will reach him tomorrow morning."

Eamon searched her face as if weighing her words, but the determination in her eyes was unmistakable. Relief softened his expression, pride warming his gaze. He bent and pressed a kiss to her brow, lingering there as though sealing his vow of protection.

"I am very proud of you, Sophie," he murmured. "And I promise you this — tomorrow, should he dare to come here, you will not face him alone. I will see to it that you are protected."

Her lips curved into a fragile smile as she whispered, "Thank you, Grandfather."

His sternness eased, and a hint of mischief glimmered in his eyes as he straightened. "And now, with Mulligan banished from your path, we can at last turn our thoughts to happier matters — such as the ball. It is high time the world knows you not as a pawn in another man's schemes, but as our granddaughter, the jewel of the Fitzpatrick family."

For the first time that day Sophie's heart lifted, and she let herself imagine a future free of fear.

Late the following morning, the butler entered the parlor and announced the Duke of Limerick. All eyes turned as Liam Walsh strode into the room, composed yet purposeful. Sophie, seated near her grandmother, stiffened at the sight of him.

"What are you doing here, Your Grace?" she asked, unable to keep the edge from her voice. He inclined his head politely, though his gaze never left her face.

"I came to ensure that Lord Mulligan won't trouble you further."

Sophie folded her hands tightly in her lap. "That is considerate of you, but unnecessary. I already have more than enough protective men here. Your presence will only complicate matters."

"Complicate?" His hazel eyes glimmered with amusement as he stepped closer. "How so?"

"Lord Mulligan already entertains foolish notions about us. If he sees you here, he will think I broke off the engagement because of you."

The duke gave a lazy shrug, his lips curving in that infuriating smile. "But isn't that the truth? You might as well admit it." He winked, and Sophie's lips nearly betrayed her with a reluctant smile before she turned quickly away, fixing her eyes on her grandfather instead.

"Do you really think he will come, Grandfather? Perhaps he will let the matter rest," she asked, her voice tinged with fragile hope. Edwin Everton's face hardened.

"I am afraid not, child. Men like Mulligan rarely let go quietly. A confrontation is inevitable, and he will come to make his noise, mark my words."

Sophie pulled her shawl tighter about her shoulders, as though warding off a sudden chill. Fear pressed on her chest, stealing her breath. Rafferty, who had been silent by the hearth, stepped forward and placed himself at her side.

"Do not be afraid, Miss Everton," he said firmly, his protective tone leaving no room for doubt. "You will not be left alone with him. He will not harm you."

Sophie nodded, wishing she could draw strength from his certainty. Still, fear curled inside her like an unwelcome shadow that would not be banished.

Just before the luncheon bell, a maid hurried in and whispered to Edwin Everton. The older man's face tightened.

"The Earl of Adare is at the door," he announced grimly. The servants, under strict instructions, refused him entry, forcing him to wait out in the snow-covered courtyard. Sophie went pale, her lips parting as though to speak, but her grandfather placed a steadying hand on her arm and inclined his head toward the door.

Together, they stepped outside. The cold bit into Sophie's cheeks, but she stood tall, chin lifted in defiance as they faced the unwelcome figure.

Lord Mulligan was pacing, his breath fogging in the frigid air. His expression twisted with indignation when he saw them.

"What is this? Why am I not allowed into my own house?"

Before Sophie could answer, Edwin's voice cut through, sharp as steel. "Because you stepped far too close to my granddaughter yesterday. That will not happen again."

The earl faltered, clearly not expecting such bluntness. His gaze darted between them before settling on Sophie, his tone softening.

"Miss Everton, my apologies. My behavior was... unpardonable. But I was not myself. It was a mistake—I should never have acted so. Believe me when I say, I do not usually behave that way."

Sophie's eyes narrowed, her voice steady despite the tremor in her hands. "You would want me to believe that, wouldn't you?"

"One mishap, and you end our engagement?" His tone sharpened again, desperation creeping in.

"It was not one mishap," Sophie said coldly. "Our engagement is over. Your temper has wounded me more times than I care to count. Each time you apologized, and each time you failed me again. I will not bind myself for life to a man who knows neither respect nor true affection."

His jaw tightened. "You should at least give me another chance."

"No," she said, her voice rising with passion. "You've had chance after chance. I will marry only a man who loves me, honors me, and cherishes me. That man is not you."

Something in her tone told him she would not waver. His face hardened, remorse vanishing in an instant. With a sudden lunge, he seized for her wrists—but Rafferty was quicker. He pulled Sophie back, placing himself firmly between her and the earl.

Before the situation could escalate further, another figure joined them. Liam Walsh stepped forward, positioning himself beside Rafferty, his stance radiating challenge. His eyes glittered with restrained fury as he addressed the earl.

"Of course your so-called protector is here," Mulligan sneered, breathing through clenched teeth. "I knew he was the reason you broke our betrothal. How long, Sophie? How long have you been meeting him behind my back?"

Sophie rolled her eyes, biting back her fury. She shot a glance at Liam, who met her gaze steadily. Her expression was fierce, her eyes speaking as clearly as words: *You see? I warned you.* She moved to step forward, determined to defend herself, but both Rafferty and the duke blocked her path, unwilling to let her face the earl's wrath alone.

"Listen, Mulligan," the young duke snapped, his voice cutting through the air like a whip. His fists clenched at his sides, his body taut, ready to strike if the man so much as twitched closer.

"Stop blaming everyone but yourself for your failures. This is on you and you alone. Instead of cherishing Miss Everton—honoring her as she deserves—you chose to belittle her, to humiliate her before an entire room of witnesses. Yesterday laid you bare for what you are: a disgrace, a coward, a low creature without a shred of honor. No woman in Ireland could feel safe in your presence."

A ripple of murmurs passed among the onlookers of footmen and servants at the sharpness of his words. Sophie's breath caught, her heart pounding—both stunned and oddly moved that someone had spoken for her so fiercely.

For a moment, Lord Mulligan looked as if he might explode. His jaw worked furiously, his nostrils flared, but at last, with so many eyes upon him and the duke looming like a lion ready to pounce, he faltered. His shoulders sank. His bravado dimmed.

"Fine," he spat, his voice dripping venom as he turned his glare on Sophie. "But don't come crawling back to me later. I knew you would disgrace your father's memory. He is turning in his grave, knowing you never meant to keep the promises you made him before he died. Tell me, Sophie, was it because you hated him for arranging your marriage? Was that why you got rid of him? Was it you who murdered your parents?"

The words struck like knives. Sophie gasped, her eyes wide with shock and disbelief. For a heartbeat she could not breathe, her whole body frozen in horror.

"That is enough!" Edwin thundered, his voice reverberating through the courtyard. But the Duke of Limerick was already moving. With a snarl, he lunged forward, seizing Mulligan by the throat. His grip was iron, his face inches from the earl's, his voice low and lethal.

"Say another word against her, and I swear you won't leave this ground alive. Leave now, or we will finish this here and now."

Mulligan clawed at his hand, his eyes bulging with fury and fear. He finally staggered back as the duke released him, coughing and gasping for air. Still, he tried to salvage his pride, spitting his final venom toward Sophie.

"Well, this turn of events suits me well enough," he sneered.

"I have already sold everything your grandfather owns. The new master has been waiting eagerly, and the papers were signed this very morning. By tomorrow, you and your precious family will be tossed into the snow like beggars, with nowhere to go."

He mounted his horse in one swift, angry motion, dug his heels in, and the beast reared before plunging forward, hooves striking the snow as he fled the estate at a reckless pace.

Silence hung heavy in his wake, broken only by Sophie's sharp intake of breath. She had been holding it too long; her body trembled violently. A wave of blackness overtook her, and she crumpled to the ground before anyone could stop her.

When consciousness returned, she was lying on a settee in the sitting room. Her lashes fluttered. She opened her eyes for a moment before closing them again, too weak to keep them open. Her grandfather sat beside her, his hand warm over hers, checking her pulse with careful fingers.

"How are you feeling, my dear?" His voice was tender, though lined with worry. Her throat tightened, and tears slipped down her cheeks as she turned her face away.

"I am so sorry, Grandfather. So terribly sorry you are losing everything because of me."

"Oh, Sophie..." Edwin's voice softened. He gently stroked her hair. "We are not losing anything because of you. Do not carry that burden. Your father lost everything long ago through his own reckless choices. That weight is his, not yours. None of this is your fault."

She sobbed quietly, her frail frame trembling against the cushions. He leaned closer, his words steady and full of conviction.

"We will find a way to rise again. But understand this—what matters most to your grandmother and me is not land, not titles, not wealth. What matters most is you, Sophie. Your happiness, your freedom. You deserve a husband who worships the ground you walk on, who guards your heart as his most sacred treasure. Mulligan cares for nothing and no one but himself. If you had bound your life to him, he would have crushed your spirit and shattered your heart."

Sophie closed her eyes and pressed her lips together, his words both comforting and cutting. For the first time, she allowed herself to imagine a different kind of future—one free of Mulligan's shadow, free to hope again.

Nervous tension gripped the Everton household like a vice. No one knew what to expect, but all feared that Kenneth Mulligan's claim of having sold everything was no idle threat. Edwin had dismissed all but one protector. Only Rafferty remained, stationed faithfully in the parlor with Sophie and her grandfather, when a maid entered, pale and hesitant.

"The Earl of Adare and a Mr. Thomas Henry to see you, My Lord."

Sophie's chest tightened. Her breath came shallow and quick until Rafferty stepped behind her, steadying her with a quiet word of reassurance. Still, her hands shook as the door opened and a young man of about five-and-twenty strode in, followed by Mulligan and several constables.

Sophie clutched the back of an armchair to steady herself. "What is all this?" Her voice trembled, but her gaze locked on the stranger. "Why is Lord Mulligan here, and why are there constables?"

"Miss Everton, I presume?" The newcomer inclined his head, his tone cool and assessing. Sophie gave a reluctant nod. "Lord Mulligan is here to show me around. This is my estate now, and his presence is by my invitation."

Her lips parted in disbelief, but before she could speak, Mr. Henry continued, his expression stern, almost smug.

"The constables are here to arrest your grandfather."

Her gasp pierced the silence. The color drained from her face until she was white as a sheet. Thankfully her grandmother was absent, Edwin had wisely spared her this scene.

"Why?" Sophie demanded, her voice breaking with fury. "Why would you arrest my grandfather?"

Henry clasped his hands behind his back, unruffled. "Your father did not merely fall into debt. Before I purchased this estate, I employed investigators. Their findings were clear—Albert Everton funneled money into illegal pursuits, schemes meant to overthrow government and abolish the nobility."

"Lies!" Sophie cried, her eyes blazing.

"Not at all, Miss Everton." His words dripped with disdain. "Your father, and your mother, were anything but virtuous people."

"How dare you?" Sophie snapped, tears pricking her eyes. "How dare you malign those you never even knew? My mother would never have been part of such wickedness."

From the side, Mulligan sneered. "Yet she is dead too, isn't she, Sophie?"

"Silence, Mulligan," Henry barked. "This is no longer your concern."

Sophie's voice rose, fierce and unyielding. "Even if my father was guilty, what has that to do with my grandfather?"

"It was his fortune that funded it," Henry replied smoothly.

"He had no idea what my father used the money for."

Henry's lip curled. "Forgive me, but one does not hand over large sums without knowing their purpose."

"That only shows how little you know of family loyalty," Sophie shot back, her eyes flashing. "You trust those you love. You believe the best of them."

Henry scoffed. "Dreams and foolishness. Constables!" he ordered briskly.

"No!" Sophie leapt forward, planting herself before her grandfather. Her small frame shook, but her voice rang like steel. "You will not take him. Get out of this house!"

"Sophie," Edwin murmured, trying to calm her, but she did not move.

"You will not take my grandfather," she repeated, her chin lifting proudly. "Take me instead."

The earl and Henry both burst into cruel laughter.

"You?" Mulligan sneered. "You would trade places with your grandfather and go to Limerick Gaol? How charming."

"I mean it," Sophie said, her voice sharp with defiance.

"Sophie, enough," Edwin pleaded. "You will not sacrifice yourself." He turned to the steward. "Mr. McMahon."

Rafferty obeyed at once, wrapping his arms around Sophie's waist and holding her back as she struggled. As the constables moved toward Edwin, Sophie panicked, her cries breaking the air.

"Please—no! I have already lost my parents. Will you truly be so heartless? He is innocent. My father did these things, if they are even true, not my grandfather. He has done nothing but good his entire life."

Her eyes, wide with terror, fixed on Thomas Henry. For a long moment he studied her in silence, weighing, calculating. At last, he spoke.

"I will make you a proposal. Your grandparents may go free, without punishment or consequence. But you will remain here. With me."

"What?" Her voice cracked.

"I will give you time to know me. By the end of the year, we shall be wed."

"If you think I will let you ruin my reputation, you are mistaken."

"I swear I will not compromise you. You may keep your maid, but the steward must go."

"Don't," Rafferty warned, alarm flashing in his eyes. "It's a trap."

Henry's grin was sharp as a blade. "If you refuse, Baron Everton will be arrested, and your grandmother exiled."

"When?" Sophie whispered.

"This afternoon."

Tears threatened, but she steadied her voice. "Will I be allowed to visit them?"

"No. You will not even know where they are until I deem your family's debt repaid. You may leave the house and grounds, but if you attempt to flee or confide in neighbors, your grandfather will hang."

"This is monstrous," Rafferty roared.

"What will it be, Miss Everton?"

She forced herself to stand tall though her insides quaked. "You swear to stay away from me, and my grandparents go free?"

"Yes."

"And how shall I know you will not betray me, arrest him behind my back?"

"You have my word. To prove my honor, I will allow your grandparents one letter a month."

Her heart shattered, but her course was clear. "Will you also swear that Mulligan cannot come near me, or the servants?"

Henry raised a brow. "Your servants?"

"Yes," Sophie said firmly. "He mistreats them."

Mulligan sneered, but Henry silenced him with a curt gesture. "Very well. The earl will have no authority here. McMahon may check on you daily to ensure my promises are kept."

Sophie turned to the window. Snow clouds loomed heavy, mirroring the storm inside her. She closed her eyes, drew a deep breath, and whispered, "I agree."

"Good." Henry clapped his hands once. "Mulligan, you may leave. McMahon, see that the baron and baroness are packed and gone before nightfall. I will also need to know which servants can be trusted to remain for Miss Everton's protection."

One by one, they filed out until the door clicked shut. Left alone, Sophie sank onto the settee, burying her face in her hands. At last, her tears came in torrents. Her heart had been torn into a thousand pieces.

It was nearly dark outside when Sophie stirred awake. The flames in the hearth had burned low, sending flickering shadows dancing across the walls. A few candles glowed on the mantel, their gentle light softening the room into a cocoon of quiet warmth. She blinked in confusion. At some point she must have drifted into sleep. A blanket had been laid across her, tucked neatly at the corners. She pushed herself upright, rubbing the heaviness from her eyes.

The door creaked softly, and a young maid entered carrying a bundle of firewood. Sophie recognized her instantly—the girl she had defended from Lord Mulligan's cruelty.

"Did you sleep well, Miss Everton?" the maid asked, her voice low and respectful. Sophie nodded, though her throat felt tight.

"Where is everyone?"

"Everyone has left, miss."

The words made Sophie's heart plummet. She shot to her feet, clutching the blanket in disbelief.

"Gone? My grandparents—are they gone too? I didn't even get to say goodbye."

The girl hesitated, then spoke gently, as though repeating something rehearsed. "Mr. Henry came in earlier. You were asleep, and he said you looked so peaceful he could not bear to wake you. He covered you himself and ordered the staff not to disturb you. He... he seems very kind."

Kind. Sophie's lips parted, but no words came. How could she tell this innocent maid that Thomas Henry was anything but kind? That beneath his polished manners lay threats and chains? She pressed her lips together, swallowing the bitter truth. The girl had already suffered enough.

"What is your name?" Sophie asked instead.

"Astrid, miss."

Sophie tilted her head. "That's not a name we hear often here."

The maid smiled shyly. "My parents came from Sweden. They wished me to carry something of their home with me."

"It's a beautiful name," Sophie said softly, though her heart ached too much to smile.

"Is there anything you need, miss? Shall I help you change before dinner?"

"I'm not hungry," Sophie murmured.

Astrid shifted uncertainly. "But Mr. Henry will be expecting you..."

"I'm not going," Sophie said, turning away. Her voice was cool though her chest burned. "Please, just give me a little time alone. It has been... a difficult day."

The maid bobbed into a curtsy. "Of course, Miss Everton." She set the firewood by the hearth, stirred the embers back to life, and slipped quietly from the room.

When the door clicked shut, Sophie released the breath she had been holding. She wandered toward the tall windows, pressing a hand to the cold glass as she gazed into the gardens. A handful of servants bustled about the sheds, stacking wood against the deepening winter night. Snow had begun to fall again, lazy white flakes drifting down to cover the familiar paths. Her eyes moved to the pavilion at the far end of the garden, and the sight undid her. That had been her grandparents' favorite place—a retreat for quiet talks, for laughter, for peace. Now it stood empty, its graceful frame half-shrouded in snow.

Her chest tightened, and hot tears spilled over. Why was her life a constant cycle of loss and heartache? Why was she always thrust from one trial into another, never given the chance to simply breathe and belong?

The door opened again. Sophie stiffened, quickly swiping at her tears, her back still to the intruder.

"Astrid tells me you won't be joining me for dinner?" Thomas Henry's deep voice came, low and smooth. Her heart lurched. She nodded without turning.

"That's right."

"Why not?"

"I'm not hungry." She tried to steady her voice, but the tremor of unshed tears betrayed her.

"Perhaps eating something would do you good," he suggested gently. The tone was soft, almost kind—but that gentleness unsettled her more than his threats. It was easier when he played the villain. Kindness confused her defenses.

"You didn't even let me say goodbye," she whispered, her voice raw. She turned abruptly, intending to leave the room, but he stepped forward and caught her arm. Startled, she froze as he drew her nearer.

"I didn't mean to wound you, Miss Everton," he said quietly. "I thought sleep was what you needed most. And I feared a farewell might break you even more."

Against her will, Sophie lifted her gaze to his. His hazel eyes fixed intently on her face, softened with something that looked almost like understanding. His tafia brown hair, slightly tousled, cast shadows across his brow, and the scruff along his jaw gave him a rugged edge that contrasted too sharply with the stern, dangerous man she had seen him to be.

Despite herself, Sophie's pulse quickened. He was too handsome—dangerously so. She lowered her eyes at once, retreating a step to break the spell.

"Please excuse me," she whispered, her voice scarcely audible. Without another glance, she walked past him toward the door.

"Good night, Miss Everton," he murmured behind her.

Her hand trembled on the doorknob. "Good night, Mr. Henry," she answered, and fled before he could see the war raging in her eyes.

14

Lifted from the Snow

As soon as Sophie closed the door to her bedchamber, she pressed her back against it and drew in slow, unsteady breaths. Her heart thundered, refusing to calm. She pressed a hand to her chest, certain something must be terribly wrong with her. Fever, perhaps—why else would she feel this sudden, bewildering pull toward a man who had taken everything from her?

Thomas Henry had claimed her grandparents' home, exiled her dearest relations, and even welcomed the vile Earl of Adare under his roof—yet her treacherous heart had skipped at the brush of his hand, at the warmth in his hazel eyes. It made no sense.

Why did she fear him one moment, yet feel inexplicably safe the next? Why did some quiet voice inside whisper that all would be well, that she need not fear? She shook her head, refusing to believe it. Trusting him was folly. And yet...

The past weeks had pushed her beyond endurance—each day another storm, each night a battle to keep hope alive. Joy at finally meeting her mother's parents had been so swiftly overshadowed by cruel blows that her heart felt bruised and torn. Surely it was this ceaseless upheaval, this endless swing between heartbreak and fleeting happiness that had unsettled her mind and made her heart so easily confused.

Wearily, she slipped into her nightgown and climbed beneath her blankets. Folding her hands, she whispered a prayer, her lips trembling as she sought the comfort she could no longer find in human arms.

Slowly, her heartbeat steadied, her spirit quieted. God had guided her all her life, and she clung to the certainty that He would not forsake her now. At last, with that thought, she drifted into restless, but healing, slumber.

The next morning, pale winter light filtered through the curtains. Sophie stretched and rose, drawing them open to find her room already warm and glowing. Astrid had been before her—her dress laid out neatly, a cheerful fire crackling in the grate, the air fragrant with pine.

Sophie's eyes widened. Her fireplace had been garlanded with evergreens and holly, little ribbons tied into bows, the entire chamber dressed as though a vision of Christmas had come alive.

Her lips parted in astonishment.

"What is this?"

"Oh, you're awake. Good morning, Miss Everton." Astrid's bright voice came from the doorway, her arms full of more greenery. She beamed as she set it down. "With Christmas approaching, Mr. Henry asked us to decorate the house and grounds as festively as possible. Everyone has been at it since before dawn—like children, laughing and singing as we worked. It's been such joy."

Sophie stood speechless. Her parents had always kept Christmas muted, almost austere, and even her grandparents had never gone to such lengths. Yet here, every corner seemed alive with celebration. Red bows, dried orange slices, polished apples gleaming against dark pine—it was enchanting.

A flicker of guilt pricked her. How could she admire any of this when her grandparents were gone, cast out because of Henry's bargain? But Astrid's delight was so genuine that Sophie bit back her bitterness and forced herself to smile.

Drawn by curiosity, she hurried downstairs once she was dressed. With each step, her eyes widened further. The house smelled heavenly—spiced oranges, beeswax candles, and fresh greenery. Garlands trailed from the banisters, berries shone like jewels, and every room glowed with warmth. Perhaps Thomas Henry was not a kind-hearted man. But he loved Christmas

"Good morning, Miss Everton."

The deep voice drifted up from below, startling her so completely that her foot slipped on the stair. With a gasp, she teetered, about to fall—only to find herself caught in strong arms. Thomas Henry's hands steadied her, his nearness sending a rush of heat into her cheeks.

"Careful," he said softly, his lips curving into the faintest smile.

Sophie's breath caught. "Forgive me," she gasped, stepping quickly out of his hold, her cheeks flushed. Thomas inclined his head.

"No, forgive me. I shouldn't have startled you." His gaze flicked toward the greenery and garlands. "You seem to like the decorations?"

Sophie hesitated, then nodded, a smile softening her features—her first true smile in his presence since their acquaintance began.

"It looks lovely. I've never seen a home so beautifully adorned."

"That is a shame," he murmured, studying her intently, as though her reaction mattered far more than the adornments themselves. "I grew up with this. My family never let the season pass without turning the house into a place of wonder, and I have always tried to keep the tradition alive." His eyes lingered on her face, fascinated by how the candlelight caught in her blue eyes—eyes that still held sorrow, yet glimmered with fragile hope.

"Will you join me for breakfast this morning?" he asked, his voice lower now, almost coaxing.

At once, the warmth in her face dimmed. She seemed to remember why he was here, under this roof. The spark faded, replaced by wariness. She gave a small nod but did not smile again.

They entered the breakfast room together. Thomas took his place at the head of the table, his posture composed though his thoughts were not. He watched her as she sat quietly, her gaze roaming the festively dressed chamber without truly seeing it. She stirred the food on her plate, appetite gone, her lips pressed tightly as though holding back tears.

The silence stretched until Thomas cleared his throat. "Miss Everton," he said carefully, "would you care to join me on a little adventure today?"

Her head lifted, her eyes brightening for the first time since she sat down. "Adventure?"

He gave her a small nod, pleased by her curiosity. "Yes. After seeing how much joy the decorations gave you, I thought perhaps you might like to join me in hunting down a Christmas tree."

"A Christmas tree?" she repeated, blinking. The concept

seemed foreign.

"It is a German tradition," Thomas explained, leaning forward, eager to see her reaction. "Queen Charlotte introduced it to England, and my family embraced it at once. Each year we ride into the woods, find the finest pine we can, and bring it home to decorate with ribbons, garlands, and candles. It is a beautiful sight when it is finished."

Her blue eyes widened, shimmering with sudden excitement. "Is it like the yule log tradition?"

He chuckled. "In a way. Except we want the whole tree, not just a single log to burn."

Sophie's lips curved, the spark of delight making her look younger, almost carefree. "When you say we... you mean you and I will fetch it? Not the servants?"

Thomas laughed at the eager disbelief in her voice. "Yes, we will fetch it ourselves. No servants this time."

"I can honestly say that I have never done anything like that before."

"Then it is long overdue." His words came out warmer than he intended. He forced himself to lean back, to restrain the sudden pull in his chest. He could not forget why she was here, what bound her to him. She was a complication he could ill afford. And yet, he found himself saying softly, "I would be delighted for you to join me."

Her smile returned, timid yet genuine. "Then I shall."

"Wonderful," he said, rising. "Let me fetch my coat."

When they stepped outside, the air was sharp and bracing, each breath turning into a cloud of frost. Waiting near the sleigh was

Rafferty, his watchful eyes scanning the grounds.

"Mr. McMahon, it is good to see you," Sophie said brightly, her voice carrying the first note of true cheer in days.

Rafferty's expression softened at once. "You look beautiful, Miss Everton."

Heat rushed into her cheeks. She told herself it was only the sting of the cold, yet her heart fluttered at the compliment. She wore her dark red coat, the one her grandmother had once said made her eyes shine brighter. She lowered her gaze, suddenly self-conscious, especially under the weight of Thomas's unspoken scrutiny.

"I've asked Mr. McMahon to join us on our little adventure," Thomas remarked smoothly, his eyes never leaving Sophie. "I trust that is agreeable to you?"

"Of course it is." Sophie's lips curved into a delighted smile. She very nearly twirled in the snow with girlish excitement, but caught herself just in time. Both men exchanged an amused glance, their expressions softening as they helped her into the sleigh.

It was a brilliantly cold day, the kind that bit at the cheeks yet made every breath feel crisp and alive. The winter sun shone through a pale blue sky, and the snow sparkled like a thousand scattered diamonds. The runners of the sleigh hissed softly over the frozen ground until they reached a dense part of the forest where tall pine trees stood, their branches heavy with snow.

They dismounted, and the three of them spread out to search for the perfect tree. Sophie wandered among the towering pines, her boots crunching through the snow, her breath rising in delicate clouds. A hush lay over the woods, broken only by the distant call of a bird and the occasional snap of a twig underfoot.

She stopped before a particularly large pine, its branches full and symmetrical. Tilting her head, she tried to judge its height.

"Do you think it would fit into the drawing room? Or will the ceiling be too low?"

Thomas and Rafferty came to stand beside her, surveying the tree with practiced eyes. After a thoughtful pause, Thomas nodded. "It should fit. If it proves a little too tall, we can trim the base. But I believe it will do perfectly."

Satisfied, the men set to work, taking turns with the axe. Each swing echoed through the forest, the sound sharp against the still air. Sophie left them to their task, wandering through the snowy clearing. She closed her eyes for a moment, simply savoring the quiet beauty around her—the scent of pine, the bite of cold on her cheeks, the strange but comforting sense of freedom in the wilderness.

By the time she turned back, the tree had been felled and the men were already tying it securely to the sleigh. She hurried toward them, her thoughts flitting between gratitude for such simple joy and the ache of her recent heartbreaks.

She was only a few steps away when a large bird, startled from its perch, shot out of the branches above. Its wings brushed her hair as it swept past, and Sophie gave a terrified scream. Both men spun around, alarm flashing across their faces. But when they saw the culprit, nothing more than a flustered bird, their concern dissolved into unrestrained laughter. Sophie placed her hands on her hips, feigning indignation though her lips twitched at the corners.

"Are you seriously laughing at me?"

Before either could answer, she scooped up two handfuls of snow, packed them quickly, and launched the snowballs straight at their unsuspecting faces. Her aim was true. Both men sputtered in surprise as the icy clumps burst against them, silencing their laughter at once.

Her giggle bubbled out, light and musical, until she saw the transformation on their faces—their shock turning to slow, mischievous grins. She gasped, recognizing the danger too late, and dashed toward the trees. But she wasn't quick enough.

Thomas caught her easily, his arms sweeping around her and lifting her clear off the snowy ground. Sophie squealed, half in protest, half in delight, as he held her fast. Her heart thudded wildly, and for one dangerous moment she could scarcely breathe. His hazel eyes locked onto hers, startling in their intensity, and she felt herself drawn in despite every warning voice in her mind.

The Duke of Limerick's eyes were hazel too, she reminded herself desperately—but lighter—not as dark as Mr. Henry's, whose gaze was nearly brown. And though the duke had stirred a measure of attraction in her, never had she felt this trembling, breathless pull toward him. He had vexed her to no end, yes—but why was it this man, this infuriating man, who made her heart pound so recklessly?

"That was a foolish thing to do, Miss Everton," Thomas said, his voice low, teasing yet edged with something else, something that made her pulse skip. "You know that deserves punishment?"

"You laughed at me," she countered, her lips curving into a stubborn pout. Rafferty stepped closer, his grin broad and approving.

"She has a point, Henry. That wasn't very gentlemanly of us."

Thomas narrowed his eyes but chuckled. "It seems you escape this time, young lady. But next time, I won't be so forgiving." His words carried a playful growl that sent a shiver down her spine.

15

The Spark Beneath the Mistletoe

He set her gently back on her feet, but in her haste to flee she caught her boot on a tree root and stumbled forward. Once again, she found herself caught in his strong arms, her face mere inches from his. Her cheeks flamed, hotter than any fire.

"Forgive me," she whispered, mortified. "I don't mean to be so clumsy."

His expression softened, though his grip lingered a moment too long. "Don't worry, Miss Everton. We all have days like this."

Astrid helped Sophie peel off her damp outer garments and ushered her toward a steaming bath already prepared. The fragrant water, infused with herbs and pine, welcomed her aching limbs. She sank into it with a sigh, tilting her head back, allowing herself the rare luxury of peace.

"Did you enjoy yourself, Miss Everton?" Astrid asked as she folded the clothes neatly to the side.

"It was lovely," Sophie admitted, her eyes closing as the warmth seeped through her. "The woods are beautiful in winter, perhaps even more than in summer."

The maid leaned closer, her tone suddenly conspiratorial. "And what of Mr. Henry? Was he charming? A true gentleman?"

Sophie jerked, startled by the question, and slipped beneath the water in her fluster. She resurfaced a second later, gasping for breath.

"Goodness, are you all right, Miss Everton?" Astrid cried, rushing forward.

"Yes, yes, I am fine," Sophie assured her quickly, forcing calm back into her voice. She closed her eyes, silently begging the girl not to press further. Fortunately, Astrid let the matter drop.

But Sophie's thoughts betrayed her. No matter how she tried to push them aside, her mind returned again and again to Thomas Henry—his steady hands catching her, his laughter ringing through the forest, his teasing words that left her trembling. She flushed all over, remembering how clumsy she must have seemed. Surely he thought her a silly goose, tripping over roots and screaming at birds.

Yet what unsettled her most was not her own embarrassment, but the truth she was beginning to see: her heart felt safer with him than it ever had with the Earl of Adare...or even the Duke of Limerick. Thomas Henry, the man who had forced her grandparents away, the man who had threatened her family's name, was also the one whose presence steadied her fears and set her pulse racing with a bewildering mix of dread and yearning. Why him? Why now?

Sophie sank deeper into the warm water, closing her eyes as though hiding her face from herself.

When Sophie descended the staircase that afternoon, she wore a gown of deep green silk that shimmered softly in the candlelight, the rich hue setting off the brilliance of her blue eyes. The dress embraced her slender frame with elegant simplicity, and her golden hair spilled in soft waves over her shoulders. She had no idea she was being observed.

From the shadow of a far corner, Thomas Henry stood silently, his gaze fixed upon her. The firelight caught in his dark hazel eyes as he watched her move with quiet grace, and something stirred in him he could not quite name.

Sophie entered the drawing room, her steps slowing when her eyes fell upon the pine tree. It stood in its place of honor, tall and proud, though still bare of ornament. She moved closer, breathing in the crisp scent of evergreen, her lips curving into a fleeting smile.

Thomas stepped through the doorway, his boots sounding softly against the polished floor. Sophie turned quickly, heat rushing to her cheeks when she realized he had caught her in her reverie.

"Are you feeling refreshed, Miss Everton?" His voice was low, warm, touched with eagerness.

She nodded, returning his gaze with a small smile.

"I do, thank you."

"I instructed the servants not to decorate the tree," he continued, stepping nearer. "I thought perhaps you might like to share that task with me this evening."

Her breath caught before she managed a graceful reply. "I would be delighted." She glanced away, suddenly shy, but his warm smile lingered in her mind. Sophie drifted toward the windows, seeking the cool air to steady her racing thoughts. Snow fell gently outside, turning the garden into a silver wonderland. For a moment, she drew comfort from the view—until the spell was broken by the entrance of a maid.

"The Earl of Adare and Miss Edington have arrived," the maid announced. Sophie's smile vanished at once, her stomach twisting. Thomas turned sharply, his expression hardening.

"Take them to my study."

"Yes, sir." The girl bobbed a curtsy and hurried away, relief plain on her face. Thomas turned back to Sophie, his tone softer.

"This will not take long. Please, excuse me."

She inclined her head, though her heart thudded with unease. He lingered for the briefest moment, as though reluctant to leave her, then stepped out. Almost at once Astrid slipped into the room.

"Is everything all right, Miss Everton? You look displeased."

"Lord Mulligan is here," Sophie replied grimly.

Astrid gasped, her eyes widening in fear. "Will he come in here?"

"No," Sophie reassured her quickly, realizing what terrified the girl. "Mr. Henry is receiving them in his study. You will not have to see him. Go to my room for now, Astrid, and I'll send for you once the earl is gone."

The maid's shoulders sagged in relief. "Thank you, Miss Everton." With another curtsy, she slipped away.

Sophie released a heavy sigh once she was alone again. Restlessness prickled through her. She could not simply sit and wait while Lord Mulligan prowled under the same roof. Curiosity, sharper than caution, drew her from the drawing room and down the familiar corridor toward her grandfather's old study.

The chamber had not yet been claimed by Thomas Henry, which was fortunate, for it concealed a secret Sophie had stumbled upon not long after her parents' passing, when she first came to

Ireland. Behind a row of shelves lay a hidden door, narrow and nearly invisible, leading into a cramped crawlspace.

Within it, she had discovered a curious contrivance—a panel cut into the wall and a small telescope fitted cleverly between stacks of heavy books. Her pulse quickened as she eased the panel open and pressed her eye to the glass. From here, she could see directly into Thomas's study, every word and gesture revealed.

Her fingers tightened against the wood. She wondered, as she had before, if her father—or even her grandfather—had once stood in this very place, listening to conversations never meant to be overheard. Tonight, it was her turn.

"I must say, you've transformed this house into quite a delightful place," Lord Mulligan remarked with forced politeness. "Have the servants always decorated so lavishly?"

Thomas leaned back in his chair, unruffled. "No, they have not. It's a family tradition. I thought the house would benefit from a touch of festivity. The staff have taken great joy in it, and their creativity has surpassed my expectations."

Peering through the hidden panel, Sophie noted how measured and calm Thomas sounded—so different from Mulligan's restless arrogance. She was about to allow herself the smallest smile when Mable Edington, seated far too comfortably, thrust herself into the conversation.

"And do your plans include fetching a tree, Mr. Henry?" she asked with affected sweetness. "I would dearly love to join you."

Sophie's stomach twisted. How could one woman be so shameless? Mable fluttered her lashes as if Thomas were the only man alive, though not long ago she had been tripping over herself to secure the Duke of Limerick's favor. *How many men's attention did she require to satisfy her vanity?* Chiding herself for the jealous spark that flared, Sophie pressed her lips together. *What does it matter? He means nothing to me.*

"I already procured my tree this morning," Thomas replied smoothly. Mable's lips parted in exaggerated disappointment.

"What a pity. I could still help decorate it."

"That will not be necessary," Thomas said, clipped. "Miss Everton will join me for that."

"Miss Everton?" Mable's composure cracked. Her tone sharpened. "Why should she be the one?"

"She lives here," Thomas reminded her evenly. The flush of jealousy on Mable's face was unmistakable. Her veneer of charm slipped entirely.

"Shouldn't she be with His Grace? She only seemed to have eyes for him the last time I saw her." Her voice grew shrill. "And that was after I told her that I knew of the kiss that passed between her and Lord Walsh. She was quite displeased."

Sophie's hand flew to her mouth to stifle a gasp. Why was that wicked woman still talking about it, and how had she even found out?

Lord Mulligan scoffed at the revelation, but Thomas's eyes narrowed. His interest sharpened.

"The Duke of Limerick kissed Miss Everton? In plain view?"

"Oh, not in front of everyone," Mable corrected with a sly smile.

"Then how would you know about it?" Thomas asked, suspicion plain.

"Because," Mable said, lifting her chin with triumphant malice, "one of Kenneth's servants discovered that a certain footman, who currently works for the marquess, has been pilfering from his employers. I offered him a choice: be dismissed in disgrace and face prison, or spy for me. He chose wisely. And so he reported what he saw—the duke kissing Miss Everton."

The room chilled. Mulligan shifted uncomfortably while Thomas regarded her with a stare so cool it might have frozen the fire. Then Mable's expression twisted. Her malice found a new target.

"That conniving little creature acted all innocence when I confronted her, but I know better. She has already thrown herself into the arms of that steward, Mr. McMahon. A servant!" Her eyes gleamed spitefully. "Mark my words, her next victim is you, Mr. Henry. And then—"

"Is that right?" Mulligan cut in, voice sharp with annoyance. His glare silenced her. "You accuse Miss Everton of impropriety while you yourself throw your favors around like confetti. I'd say you are far guiltier than she could ever be."

Sophie nearly laughed aloud with relief but stifled it. For once the earl's venom had been directed elsewhere, and Mable deserved every word of it.

"How dare you?" she hissed, rising half from her seat.

"What? You cannot bear the truth?" Mulligan sneered. "Sit down, Mable. Your tantrums weary me. If you cannot keep a civil tongue, I will stop taking you anywhere."

Humiliation finally silenced her. The room grew taut until Thomas broke the stillness, his tone low and steady.

"Did you bring the letters?"

"No," Mulligan answered curtly. "But I will deliver them tomorrow. Do you have the rest of the money?"

Thomas's jaw tightened. "What money? I paid for the estate,

the land, and more than your asking price."

Mulligan leaned forward, eyes glinting. "Yes, and yet Miss Everton's company was not part of our arrangement. If you wish to keep her, I expect compensation."

Thomas rose slowly, his height and composure making the earl look petty. "Attempt to extort me again," he warned, "and I will have the authorities at your door within the hour. Consider this your only warning."

The earl's lips twisted. "Fine. I will return tomorrow afternoon."

Sophie slipped from her hiding place as quietly as she had entered and hurried back to the drawing room, her pulse still racing. She snatched up a book, though her eyes refused to focus on the words, and tried to steady her breathing.

Several minutes later, Thomas entered. His gaze found her at once, and he seated himself opposite, studying her in silence until she grew restless.

"What?" she demanded at last, a shade too sharply.

"I was merely thinking how very different you are from Miss Mable Edington."

Her head snapped up, eyes flashing. "Do not compare me to that woman. She is vile, manipulative, and false. She treats affections as though they were toys."

Thomas's lips curved into a faint grin. "Do I hear a hint of jealousy?"

Color rushed into Sophie's cheeks. "I—I did not mean it that way," she stammered, tearing her gaze away.

"Do not worry," he said smoothly. "I agree with you. And between us, you are infinitely more beautiful."

Her head jerked up again, heat blazing in her face. He winked, and her composure nearly fractured. If she did not leave at once, he would see far too clearly how deeply he unsettled her. Rising quickly, she set the book aside.

"Please excuse me. I must check on Astrid. The girl was shaken when she learned the earl was here."

Thomas's smile vanished instantly. "Did Mulligan harm her?"

Sophie nodded gravely. "He struck her—for a simple mistake. When I asked if it had happened before, she admitted it had. I sent her to gather her things and meet Rafferty outside. I would not leave her in that man's service."

Fury darkened Thomas's expression. "You are brave, Miss Everton. But were you not afraid he would turn his violence on you?"

"I was," she admitted softly. "And he did—not with his fists, but with something worse. He tried to... compromise me in the worst way possible. Humiliate me. Rafferty stopped him just in time."

Thomas's jaw clenched, outrage flashing in his eyes. "Then I understand completely why you cannot endure him near you."

Sophie gave a faint nod, her throat tight. Without another word, she turned and slipped from the room, her heart pounding too wildly to endure his gaze any longer.

That evening, they decorated the Christmas tree together. Astrid and two other maids were present, their soft laughter mingling with the rustle of pine branches and the glow of candlelight gleaming against glass baubles. When at last the final ribbon was tied and the star carefully fixed upon the top, Sophie stepped back, her eyes wide with wonder.

The tree was breathtaking—its branches shimmered with gold ribbons, dried oranges, and berries strung with care. Yet the beauty of it brought a sudden ache to her chest. Her grandparents should have been there, admiring it beside her. The thought threatened to undo her, so she quickly bade everyone goodnight and hurried upstairs before her composure gave way.

She had barely flung herself upon her bed before the tears came. They fell hot and fast as she buried her face in the pillow, muffling the sound of her grief. She missed them desperately, and though her heart could not deny the strange, steady pull she felt toward Thomas Henry, no man—not even one as compelling as he—could fill the void of family.

Close to midnight, her eyes still stinging, Sophie slipped from her chamber and crept down the stairs. Her heart was restless, too bruised for sleep. The house was hushed, the servants long gone to bed, but the drawing room still glowed faintly. She slipped inside, longing for solitude with the tree.

The fire crackled low in the hearth, its light warming the shadows. Sophie knelt to add another log, then drifted to the tree, her fingers brushing the pine needles as though to reassure herself it was real. The fragrance of evergreen, wood smoke, and the faint spice of dried fruit wrapped around her like a cloak.

She moved to the window. Snowflakes tumbled softly from the night sky, silver in the moonlight. Her lips curved in a fragile smile. Snow, firelight, the glittering tree—it was all so peaceful, so achingly beautiful that for the first time that day, she felt a measure of comfort. Closing her eyes, she drew in a steadying breath, willing herself to believe in that moment of calm.

When the fire burned low again, she turned reluctantly toward the door—and almost collided headlong into Thomas Henry. Her gasp escaped before she could stop it, and she raised her hand to her lips. He steadied her instinctively, his hand firm on her arm, his gaze searching hers.

"Forgive me," he murmured, his voice low. "I did not mean to startle you."

"It's all right," she whispered, still breathless. "I could not sleep. But the room is yours now."

"You don't have to leave," he said softly, his eyes lingering on her face. "I won't be in your way."

She froze beneath his gaze. A stray curl had slipped loose across her cheek, and before he could think better of it, his fingers brushed it gently behind her ear. The touch was feather-light, yet Sophie trembled beneath it.

"I do have to leave," she said in a hushed voice, her throat tight. "We shouldn't be here—not together, not alone." But her feet did not move. Her wide eyes betrayed her own uncertainty, caught between propriety and the pull of his nearness.

They stood in the threshold, the firelight flickering at their backs. Thomas tilted his head slightly, then lifted his hand to raise her chin. Above them, a sprig of mistletoe hung from the archway, its pale berries gleaming in the dim light.

Sophie's eyes darted upward, then back to his. She shook her head faintly, her breath unsteady.

"It's tradition," he said softly, his voice roughened with longing.

"Please, Thomas," she whispered, her protest barely more than a plea. "We are not even engaged."

"But we are to be married at the end of the year," he reminded her, his voice hoarse. Still she shook her head.

"We will regret this."

Yet the hesitation in her voice, the faint quiver of her lips, betrayed her. She wanted him to kiss her, he could feel it. Or perhaps he only wanted so desperately to believe it.

"I don't think we will," he murmured. Slowly, inexorably, he lowered his face toward hers. His lips brushed hers, tentative at first, a whisper of warmth that sent a shiver down her spine. Then, as if restraint shattered in both of them, the kiss deepened. Sophie's breath caught as his arms closed around her, strong and unyielding, drawing her against the hard wall of his chest. His warmth engulfed her, his heartbeat thundering beneath her palms as her hands rose to clutch at his coat.

The world seemed to fall away—the hush of the falling snow, the dim flicker of firelight, even the ache of her grief—until there was only this: his mouth on hers, fierce and desperate, tempered with tenderness that undid her completely.

Her lips parted, and he kissed her more fully, his breath mingling with hers, stealing reason and leaving only the wild rush of sensation. His hand slid along the curve of her back, holding her close, while the other framed her cheek, his thumb stroking lightly as though to soothe even as his passion threatened to consume them both.

Sophie trembled, caught between shock and surrender, every nerve alight. She had been kissed before—stolen, mocking kisses meant to humiliate her—but never like this. This was no claim of possession, no reckless game. This was hunger, reverence, and longing all at once, and it left her breathless. For one blissful moment, she let herself yield, melting into him, her heart soaring with an intensity that terrified her.

At last, the kiss softened. His lips gentled against hers,

lingering, as though he could not bear to let her go. With effort, Sophie pressed her hands against his chest, easing herself back though her knees trembled with weakness.

"We need to stop," she whispered, her voice shaking. Thomas rested his forehead against hers, his breath uneven, and his chest rising hard beneath her palms.

"I know," he admitted, his voice husky. His hand lingered at her waist, reluctant to release her.

Silence stretched, heavy with what had just passed. Then, with a faint, unsteady smile, he murmured, "When shall I speak to your grandfather and ask for your hand in marriage?"

The absurdity of the question in such a moment broke the spell, and Sophie gave a soft, breathless laugh. Her cheeks burned as she stepped back, her heart racing too wildly to bear.

"Goodnight, Thomas," she whispered, her voice soft but firm.

"Goodnight, Sophie," he replied, his tone low and full of meaning. She turned and fled up the stairs, her hand pressed over her pounding heart, knowing with trembling certainty that one kiss beneath the mistletoe had changed everything.

Sophie woke with a smile she could not quite school. Snow muffled the world beyond her windows. Night had laid down a white hush, and morning had polished it to a glittering sheen. Astrid slipped in with a curtsy and a tray.

"You must have had a wonderful dream to be glowing like that. Your whole face is shining with happiness."

Heat rose to Sophie's cheeks. "Yes. It was...beautiful." *It was not a dream,* her treacherous heart whispered. It was the memory of warm hands, of laughter by lamplight, of a kiss beneath winter-green.

Astrid helped her dress, chattering cheerfully about the kitchen maids' arguments over garlands and the footmen's pride in perfectly tied bows. Sophie let the words wash over her, though her thoughts strayed elsewhere.

When she was ready, she descended—and paused. The breakfast room was empty. Thomas was nowhere to be seen. Low voices drifted from his study. The smile slipped. Curiosity, and something sharper, pulled her down the corridor toward the hidden panel she had discovered only the day before. She eased the latch and slipped into the narrow void behind the bookshelf.

Through the slim viewing slit, the world beyond assembled itself like a stage: Thomas behind his desk, Lord Mulligan sprawled insolently in a chair, and Mable Edington upright and predatory, her smile sharp as a knife. Had not Mulligan said he would come in the afternoon?

"You're not even listening," Mable pouted, snapping her fan closed. "What is wrong with you today?"

"Don't tell me you've fallen for our little prisoner princess," Mulligan sneered. "Perhaps leaving her here alone was not the cleverest idea. Remember what you promised me, Henry."

Thomas leaned back, careless, a faint grin playing at his mouth. "I've not forgotten, Mulligan. And no, I'm not falling for her. I merely romanced her a little so she'd trust me. Remarkably simple, really. Who knew boughs and baubles, and a jaunt for a tree, could soften her up so nicely?"

16

When the Mask Slips

The words struck Sophie like a blow. Her hand flew to her mouth as she stumbled against the paneling. The narrow space seemed suddenly airless. The warm, impossible hope that had carried her into this morning cracked straight through the middle.

Fool, she told herself savagely. *You little fool.* She forced herself to breathe, to be still, to listen. Running would reveal her. Staying might save her. It took all her strength to swallow the tears burning her eyes and the sob rising in her throat. *Never again,* she vowed, fingers digging into the rough wood. *Never again will I be made a jest of. Whatever game is being played, I will not be its pawn.*

Out in the study, Thomas's gaze flicked—swift as a hawk's—toward the bookcase, as if he'd heard the faint scrape of her shoe. Sophie froze, every muscle taut. After a beat, he looked away, his face once more bored and indolent.

"Here are the letters," Mulligan said, tossing three sealed envelopes onto the desk. "See that she doesn't read them before I've had my say. After what she's done to me, I intend to watch her face when she learns the truth."

Mable snorted. "What she's done? She merely called off an

engagement. I fail to see the tragedy."

Thomas cut across them, brisk now. "Enough. Is everyone already at the meeting place?"

"Yes," Mulligan replied, rising. "Only you two are missing."

"We will be there," Thomas said, gathering the envelopes with a practiced hand before leaving them squarely in the center of his desk. "Come, I'll see you out."

Their footsteps receded down the corridor. Sophie waited—counted to ten, to fifty—until silence deepened and the house seemed to exhale. Then she slipped from the hidden recess, lifted the study latch with a thief's care, swept the three envelopes from the blotter, and vanished back through the secret door, her pulse hammering.

Once Sophie reached her chamber, she shut the door and turned the key with trembling fingers. Her breath came fast. Her heart hammered so violently she thought it might burst from her chest. She stared at the three envelopes. Each bore her name in familiar, elegant script. They had been meant for her, hidden from her, and now they were finally in her hands.

Her knees threatened to give way, but she forced herself to sit and tore open the first missive. Her breath caught. It was her mother's handwriting. She traced the letters with a fingertip as though the touch might conjure her presence. Inside was a copy of the marriage contract signed by her father and the Earl of Adare. Attached was a small note, hastily scrawled:

I don't trust Lord Mulligan. Here is a copy in case he tries to back out of my conditions.

A chill ran through Sophie. Just as she had feared, the contract made clear—she was to be married on Christmas Eve. Her fingers shook as she set it aside and reached for the second letter. It was brief, but each word pierced straight into her soul:

Sophie,

I want you to know that no matter what happens, we love you. Don't believe everything that is said about your father. He made mistakes and ruined many things, but he wasn't as bad as some people might want you to believe. Talk to both your grandparents. They know the entire story.

Love,

Mama

Tears blurred Sophie's vision. She pressed the letter to her chest and closed her eyes, feeling the ache of her mother's love across the impossible gulf of death. The certainty in those words—that her mother had known she might never see her again—broke Sophie's heart anew.

Her hands trembled as she opened the third letter. This one was longer; the script was hurried, desperate.

Dearest Sophie,

When you receive this, take it to your grandfather immediately. Your father put in his will that your grandparents have no right to interfere with the contract and no say over you, but something has occurred that changed his mind.

We are unsure if we have time to get the will changed, but this proves that your grandparents have every right to take charge. I fear we will not be alive for much longer, which is why I sent you to your sister for a few days. We thought about running away, but our house is constantly being watched, and we didn't want to give them any cause to harm you.

Your father discovered that Kenneth Mulligan is not the earl. The true earl is in France at present. The man pretending to be him is Jack Murphy, the earl's former steward. Your father overheard Jack's friends speaking in the pub, and when he investigated, he discovered the truth. But unless we can secure evidence or a confession, no one will believe us.

We have informed several nobles and the authorities and asked them to contact my father if this letter never reaches you.

Be careful, Sophie. Jack plans to move to Ireland to pose as the nephew of an earl there. The old man is dying and has not seen his kin in years. Your father has written to France to alert the true earl, but whether the letter will be read, we cannot know. Jack Murphy and his conspirators plan to kill him the moment he sets foot in Ireland. Once Jack establishes himself there, it will be nearly impossible to expose him.

I love you, Sophie, and I am so proud of the young lady you have become. Your father, though he did not show it well, loved you too. Please give my parents a chance. They can tell you more than I am able to write.

With all my love,

Mama

Sophie gasped, but then noticed another note attached to the back of the letter.

The reason your grandparents have lost their tenants is because of Jack. He threatened them with ruin if they refused to move to the old earl's lands. He is determined to destroy your father's family because your father discovered the truth.

Sophie read the page twice, then a third time, as if repetition might make the meaning less terrible. The letters in her lap blurred. The room tilted. Jack Murphy. A false earl. A plot to murder the real man. Everything she had suspected—secrets, threats, the sudden ruin of her grandparents—tangled into a cold, furious knot in her stomach.

She dropped the letters on the table and burst into uncontrollably sobs. Betrayal, danger, death—the web was darker and deeper than she had ever imagined. A sound in the corridor startled her. Footsteps on the stairs.

She gasped, folding the letters with frantic haste and shoving them into the pocket of her dress. Her heart pounded like a drum as she wiped her tears, desperate to look composed. She glanced wildly around the room, searching for a decoy. Snatching a few old papers from her desk, she folded them to resemble what she had just hidden and left them conspicuously atop the table. Then she slipped her father's little dagger into her coat pocket, its weight a small comfort.

A sharp knock rattled the door. She froze.

"Sophie—it's Thomas. May I come in?"

"No!" Her voice was high, panicked.

"Come now, Sophie. I only want to talk."

"I don't care. Go away." She heard the latch rattle—he was testing the lock. Her pulse raced. She darted to the window, throwing it open to the winter air.

"Sophie, open the door." His voice was low now, coaxing.

"No!" She pulled on her coat and gloves with frantic speed and set one foot on the sill, ready to climb down to the tree below. But before she could move, the lock clicked. The door swung wide, and Thomas was inside. She tried to scramble out, but he was too quick. His hand caught her, dragging her back.

"What do you think you're doing?" His tone was sharp, but his grip unyielding.

"Getting away from you."

"You promised, Sophie. You promised you wouldn't run."

"And you promised not to lie to me. Look at you now—breaking into my chamber, deceiving me at every turn. You're nothing but a fabulist."

His gaze flicked to the letters lying on the desk. A shadow passed over his face. "Why couldn't you leave it alone? You weren't meant to see those."

"They were mine. Addressed to me. I had every right."

"It doesn't matter anymore. You're coming with me."

"No." Her glare was pure fire. "I will not."

"Sophie," his voice tightened, "don't make this harder. I can carry you if I must."

She stood her ground, fury making her seem taller than she was. He reached for her arm, only for her to seize a vase from the table and hurl it at his head. He ducked just in time. She bolted for the door, skirts whipping around her legs. But he was faster. He caught her, turned her, and in one swift motion lifted her over his shoulder.

"Let me go! Somebody—help me!" she cried, striking his back with her fists.

"No one will hear you," he said grimly. "The servants are gone. I gave them the day off."

The words froze her blood. She had trapped herself. In trying to protect her grandfather, she had walked willingly into her enemy's hands.

Sophie's mind raced. Then she remembered the dogs. Had the servants taken them when they left? Usually, when not roaming outside, they slept by the kitchen hearth, spoiled with scraps and treats.

She let out a sharp, piercing whistle. Thomas jolted at the sound, caught off guard. Within seconds, two barking hounds burst through the kitchen door, teeth bared, and their deep growls shaking the walls. They lunged straight at him.

With Sophie still over his shoulder, Thomas staggered into the drawing room, the dogs snapping at his heels. He maneuvered quickly, slammed the door behind them, and turned the key, trapping the animals inside. Their furious barking echoed as he carried Sophie out into the cold.

Outside, two familiar faces awaited—Herbert Boyle and Declan Moore. The same brutes who had tried to abduct her weeks earlier. Sophie's stomach lurched. Of course. They had never gone far. They were still in the service of the false earl.

Without ceremony, Thomas handed her over. The men bound her wrists with coarse rope, gagged and blindfolded her, then lifted her onto a waiting sleigh. Someone climbed onto the coachman's seat, and with a harsh crack of the whip, the horses lunged forward.

Sophie sat rigid, her body shaking—not with fear, but with rage. Her heart ached so violently it felt torn in two. Thomas's nearness beside her was unbearable. How could she have trusted him? How could she have been so wrong about someone who had seemed so... different?

When the sleigh jolted to a stop, the men hauled her down and carried her into a building. The ropes were cut, the gag and blindfold torn away.

Blinking in the sudden light, Sophie realized where she was—her grandfather's chapel. And waiting for her stood Jack Murphy, Mable Edington, and a clergyman.

"What is this?" Sophie demanded, her voice fierce despite the tremor in it.

"We are getting married today," Jack declared with a triumphant grin.

"No," she hissed, springing to her feet. "I will never agree to that."

Laughter erupted around her, cruel and mocking.

"You don't have a choice, sweet Sophie," Jack sneered. "And now that I know you are the granddaughter of the Duke of Kilkenny, it pleases me even more."

Her eyes blazed. "The duke will have you hanged for this! You're doing this out of spite because my mother saw through your lies. And when my father discovered you were nothing but Jack Murphy, a servant pretending to be the Earl of Adare, you silenced them both!"

For a split second, Jack blanched. His eyes darted to Thomas. "You let her read the letters?"

Thomas shook his head tightly. "No. She stole them."

"You sneaky little wench," Jack spat, his face contorted with fury.

"The letters were addressed to me," Sophie shot back coldly. "You cannot steal what already belongs to you. You are the thief, not I."

Then she rounded on him, her voice sharp as a blade. "Tell me—did you murder my parents yourself, or did you send these cowards?" She glared at Boyle and Moore, who shifted uneasily.

Before either man could answer, Mable interjected with venom.

"Those fools? They're useless. They couldn't even succeed in kidnapping you. Jack was already on his way to Ireland, so I handled it. I slipped into your parents' home and poisoned their tea. They died just as I intended."

Sophie gasped, horror mingling with fury. "And who are you, Mable Edington?"

Mable's lips curled into a mocking smile. "Jack's sister."

Sophie's blood ran cold. "Sister? Why drag me into this? I had nothing to do with you."

"You naïve little simpleton," Mable sneered. "This is about vengeance. About punishing everyone who ever crossed us. After the real Earl of Adare left for France, we were hired by a duke and followed him to Scotland. He caught Jack in his chambers and accused him of theft. Jack was dismissed, and so was I. We made sure that duke paid for it with his life. Then his daughter—Jack married her, but she discovered the truth. She had to be silenced as well."

Sophie's stomach churned, bile rising in her throat. But Mable's voice carried on, gleeful.

"From there, we went to London. Your father was drowning in debt, and Jack saw his chance. We only meant to take your grandparents' estate. But then Jack saw you and decided he wanted you for his wife. Your father agreed all too easily. Now that I've met you, I understand why."

"You're vile," Sophie whispered, trembling with disgust.

Mable's grin sharpened. "When your father discovered Jack's secret—that he was not the earl at all—he threatened to expose us. We silenced him. Your mother suspected us from the start, so she had to die as well."

Sophie turned on Jack, her eyes blazing. "And then you came here to Ireland and pretended to be the nephew of a dying earl?"

Jack smirked. "Exactly. The old fool recognized me as nephew's steward, but his death was expected. No one questioned it. A quick end, and I had what I wanted."

17

A Hunt Concluded, A Heart Decided

"**Y**ou are worse than the devil," Sophie spat. "Both of you. Murdering the innocent because they dared to call you what you are."

"That's enough," Jack snapped, yanking her against him. "It's time. Mr. Edwards—begin."

The clergyman stammered through the opening words of the ceremony. Sophie struggled, clawing at Jack's grip.

"Why?" she demanded, her voice breaking. "Why marry me, when you mean to kill me anyway?"

"Because your grandfather will pay to keep you alive, you as his heir," Jack said with a sneer. "He has money enough to buy our freedom. Once we have it, we'll tell him you're already my wife. Then you'll be of no use. A divorce would cause a scandal."

Sophie's mind raced. "You are a fool," she said through gritted teeth. "I am not an heir. You killed my father before he could change his Will. My grandfather cannot name me his heir until I come of age. I have no title, no wealth. I am simply Sophie Everton."

Shock flickered across Jack and Mable's faces. But Jack recovered quickly, his jaw hardening.

"He will pay nonetheless—for his precious granddaughter's

life." He pulled her tighter, nodding at the clergyman to continue. Sophie struggled with all her might, but his grip was iron.

The words of the ceremony had barely begun when the chapel doors crashed open. Footsteps thundered in—constables, footmen, and at their head, Rafferty.

In the chaos, Sophie acted. Her fingers flew to the dagger concealed in her pocket. With all her strength, she drove it into Jack's leg. He howled, collapsing to one knee, his grip loosening. Sophie tore free, skirts flying, and sprinted past the guards. The cold air and cloudy sky met her like a promise as she burst out of the chapel and into freedom.

"Miss Everton was right, Murphy. You are worse than the devil!" The words rang like thunder as the true Earl of Adare strode into the chapel, his presence commanding every eye. At his side entered the Duke of Kilkenny, tall and dignified, his lined face burning with righteous fury, and just behind him, the Duke of Limerick, his expression cold and unyielding.

Jack Murphy's triumphant smirk faltered. His eyes widened in disbelief. "What—what are you doing here, My Lord? You weren't supposed to arrive for another two days." His voice cracked, betraying the first edge of fear.

The earl's mouth curved in a grim smile. "We've been watching you for a long time, Murphy—tracking your every step. You've made a career out of deceit and bloodshed, but this time your arrogance betrayed you. Did you truly think you were beyond reach? That we would sit idly by while you paraded yourself as a nobleman?"

Jack's face blanched. "I—I was told it was safe."

"Yes," the earl replied coolly, "because you trusted the wrong people. Several of those you counted as friends—your so-called allies—have been working for us all along, feeding us your every word, and your every plan. And today, you sealed your own fate." He turned his head slightly, nodding to the clergyman.

"Then why wait?" Mable shrieked, her voice sharp as shattered glass. Her eyes blazed with venom as she glared at the newcomers. "Why didn't you arrest us sooner?"

The earl's gaze hardened. "Because we needed more than accusations. We needed your own words, your confessions, spoken aloud in the presence of witnesses. Miss Everton"—he gestured toward Sophie's empty chair, his tone softening for an instant—"did the work for us without even knowing it. She drew every vile truth from your lips. And now, you stand condemned by your own boasting."

The Duke of Kilkenny's hand tightened on the top of his cane, his voice rumbling with restrained wrath.

"You dared to use my granddaughter as a pawn. You dared to poison and deceive, to kill without remorse. There will be no mercy for the likes of you."

A ripple of unease swept through the chapel. Boyle and Moore exchanged anxious glances. Even Jack's bravado crumbled beneath the weight of so many accusing eyes.

Rafferty's sharp gaze swept the room, ensuring every conspirator was covered by armed constables. But then, out of the corner of his eye, he caught a glimpse of motion—the back door creaking open, Sophie's figure darting out of the building.

For a heartbeat, relief surged through him—she was free,

beyond the villains' reach. But when he met his partner's eyes across the chaos, no words were needed. Both men understood at once.

They shoved through the press of footmen and constables, slipping out into the cold after her.

Sophie was running blind, her gown tangling about her legs, but desperation lent her wings. Snow crunched beneath her hurried steps, her breath rising in frantic white clouds against the dark winter air. And Rafferty knew—they had to reach her before someone else did.

Despite the weight of her long dress, Sophie fled across the snow with surprising speed, her breath puffing out in white clouds. Behind her, Thomas's voice cut through the stillness, calling her name—pleading—but she refused to listen. She would not be fooled again. Fury and despair pounded in her chest as she pressed forward.

Realizing he could not catch her head-on, Thomas veered into the trees, circling through the underbrush until he was ahead of her. Just as she darted past, he stepped into her path and seized her in one swift motion.

Sophie shrieked, thrashing wildly in his grip. "Why can't you leave me alone?"

"Please, Sophie, just listen to me," he urged, trying to tilt her chin so their eyes might meet.

"No!" she snapped, twisting away, her body rigid with defiance. "I will never listen to you again. I know what you did—you played me. You used your charm, your fine words, and your looks, to make me trust you. But the game is over." She struck him with her fists, desperate to break free, but his strength was unyielding.

At last, Thomas wrapped his arms firmly around her, holding her close until her struggling slowed. Her resistance faltered, tears spilling down her cheeks as she choked out, "Why do you insist on torturing me? I've lost everything—everything. My grandparents' home, their dignity... and now even my peace of mind. What more do you want from me? I have nothing left to give." Her voice cracked on the last word.

His tone softened. "If you would only hear me out, it would all make sense. None of what you believe is true."

"Of course," she said bitterly, her tears streaking her face. "It's all just a dream. Any moment now, I'll wake from this nightmare."

"No, Sophie," he said gently, turning her by the shoulders so she could no longer avoid him. "I wasn't trying to hurt you. Please, believe me. I am not who you think I am."

The instant their eyes met, her defenses crumbled. She broke down and wept, sagging against his chest.

"Please... leave me be," she begged between sobs. "I need time to myself. Why can't you understand that?"

He held her tightly, his own voice thick with regret. "I am so sorry you were caught in this. I never wanted you to be hurt. What you overheard with Jack Murphy, it wasn't the truth. I only pretended loyalty so he would trust me. We've been after him for months, ever since your parents were killed. Your grandfather wanted justice, Sophie. He reached out to the true Earl of Adare in France, and together they began their hunt. Rafferty was invaluable—he once served as a constable and spy. We had to make Murphy believe he was safe. It was the only way to bring him down."

Her sobs gradually eased. She searched his face, tears clinging to her lashes. "Then... who are you really?"

A faint smile tugged at his lips as he gazed into her eyes. "I am Liam Ronan Walsh, Duke of Limerick."

The name struck her like a slap. Sophie froze, outrage flaring anew. She shoved at him with all her strength.

"Do you take me for a fool? You expect me to believe such nonsense? Lord Walsh is a great nobleman. I know who he is, and you are not him."

"I know how it sounds," Liam said steadily, refusing to release her, "but I speak the truth."

Her voice was sharp with scorn. "I am done with your lies. Let me go this instant."

"What can I do to prove it to you?"

"Nothing. You cannot—because it is not true."

"Oh, but it is, Miss Everton," came a familiar voice. Rafferty stepped from the shadows of the trees, his expression calm, and his smile reassuring. Sophie turned to him in disbelief.

"Then explain this to me, Mr. McMahon. If he is truly Lord Walsh, then who has been parading as the duke all this time?"

Rafferty's smile deepened. "His twin brother."

"What?"

Liam sighed. "It is complicated, but it is the truth. When Rafferty became entangled in this case, I came here under an assumed name to gain Murphy's confidence. My brother Killian and I... we switched places."

Sophie blinked, her heart hammering. "I don't understand."

Rafferty stepped forward. "Killian and Liam may be twins, but they are as different as night and day. Liam is careful, deliberate—a strategist. Killian is bold, impulsive, and sometimes reckless. When we needed someone to infiltrate Murphy's circle, the choice was clear. Killian remained in Limerick, and Liam became the man you knew as Thomas Henry. It was the only way to keep you safe and unravel this web."

Her eyes searched Liam's face, desperate for truth. "Did we meet before you came to Everton estate?"

Liam nodded slowly. "Once. The afternoon Boyle and Moore tried to abduct you. I was there. And when Killian and I switched roles, it was to protect you—from Murphy, and from further confusion."

"So..." Sophie hesitated, her cheeks warming as memory struck. "The man who constantly tormented and vexed me, who dared to kiss me without permission—that was your brother?"

Liam's grin was boyish now, his eyes gleaming. "Yes. That was Killian."

Sophie's brows lifted, scandal and relief mingling. "Shameless."

"Indeed," Rafferty said with a chuckle. "Killian is accustomed to women indulging his arrogance because he is an earl, the son of the Marquess of Tipperary. But you, Miss Everton, did not yield. You put him in his place. And for that, he deserved every ounce of your wrath."

A reluctant blush touched Sophie's cheeks as Rafferty winked at her. Still shaken, she looked between the two men.

"But how could I not have noticed? You are brothers, twins even, and you share the same blood."

"It is easy to miss," Rafferty assured her. "They go to lengths not to resemble each other, and their natures are so different that most never guess. Killian cast aside his disguise when they switched again, and Liam resumed his true self."

"You also never saw us side by side," Liam added softly, his hand brushing her arm with a gentleness that made her pulse quicken.

"And you never imagined Liam could be a duke," Rafferty said knowingly. "You thought him merely a wealthy stranger seizing your grandparents' estate. You assumed much, but not the truth." Sophie's breath caught as her gaze lingered on Liam. Everything she thought she knew about him was unraveling. And yet... deep inside, something told her he was speaking from the heart.

Sophie suddenly became aware that Liam was still holding her. Her breath caught and her face flushed scarlet. She lowered her gaze, unable to meet his eyes. He only smiled, clearly amused by her fluster. The more she shifted, the more firmly he drew her against him, as if he could read every thought running through her mind.

"Your Grace," she whispered, voice soft and uncertain, "this is not proper. You shouldn't be holding me like this."

He bent his head closer, his breath warm against her temple. "It's Liam, and we already kissed," he murmured. "Tell me, Sophie, do you truly dislike being in my arms?"

Her lips parted, but no words came. Her heart thundered too loudly. "That's... that's not what I meant," she stammered, still refusing to look at him. "We are not engaged. If my grandfather saw us—"

"—he would wholeheartedly approve," came a deep, familiar voice behind them. Sophie spun around, cheeks aflame. Her grandfather's eyes twinkled with amused knowledge as he stepped into the path.

"I was hoping you and Liam would find your way to each other," Eamon Fitzpatrick said warmly. "Our families united at last, it is what your mother would have wished."

Sophie lowered her eyes, mortified. "He has not asked me,

Grandfather."

"Oh, well, if that is all that troubles you, we can remedy that at once," Liam said with a playful gleam. To Sophie's shock, he released her just long enough to sink gracefully to one knee in the snow. Her blush deepened until she thought her skin might catch fire.

"Not here," she whispered urgently, trying to tug him back to his feet. "Please, Liam, this is not the place—"

Her grandfather chuckled, clearly enjoying her discomfiture.

"What? You don't wish me to propose in front of your grandfather?" Liam teased, looking up at her with exaggerated innocence. "I cannot imagine a more perfect witness."

Sophie buried her face in her hands for a moment, wishing the ground would swallow her.

"I'm not certain that I am ready," she mumbled, eyes downcast.

"You are more than ready, Sophie," her grandfather said firmly. "Now, let him ask the question. He cannot stay kneeling there forever. If it eases you, I shall look away."

At that Sophie let out a breathless giggle despite herself. Slowly she raised her head. When her eyes met Liam's, his expression was so earnest, so tender, that the last of her resistance dissolved.

Taking her hand in both of his, Liam's voice grew steady and rich with feeling.

"Sophie, you have come into my life and overturned everything I thought I knew. You have challenged me, bewildered me, and stolen my heart so completely that I cannot imagine a day without you. I long to love you, to protect you, to cherish you for the rest of my life. My heart is yours, now and always. Will you do me the honor of becoming my wife?"

The world narrowed to his dark hazel eyes and her own blue

ones. Sophie's breath trembled. A radiant smile broke across her face. She nodded, small and resolute. Liam rose and gathered her into his arms as if he would never let go. Her laugh rang out, mingling with the sound of her grandfather's footsteps approaching.

"And you have my blessing," Eamon said, his voice thick with emotion. "Congratulations, my dear. And to you, Liam, I could not be more delighted."

Sophie leaned against Liam's chest, heart soaring, and for the first time in what felt like forever, she truly belonged.

18

A Christmas of Promises

When Liam and Sophie were finally alone again, the world seemed to hush around them. He lifted her chin with a touch so gentle it sent shivers coursing through her, then claimed her lips in a kiss full of fervent longing. His mouth moved against hers with slow, deliberate passion, deepening until her heart raced wildly and her knees nearly gave way beneath her.

Yet she felt no fear of falling—his arms held her securely, strong and unyielding, as though he would never let her go. Breathless and dazed, Sophie drew back at last, though she remained pressed close to him. He rested his forehead tenderly against hers, their breath mingling, and his gaze soft with unspoken devotion.

"Thank you," she whispered, her voice trembling. "Thank you for making this terrible ordeal a little sweeter. The way you had the house decorated, the joy of choosing the Christmas tree together... I cannot tell you what it meant to me."

He brushed the tip of his nose against hers in a fleeting caress. "I could see how much you needed something to lift your spirit, to remind you that beauty and joy still exist. You've endured so much, Sophie. I would not have you remember this season only as a nightmare."

Her lips curved, her eyes lighting with a mischievous spark.

"Did you hang the mistletoe in the doorway on purpose?"

His grin was boyish, irresistible—and before answering, he stole another kiss, lingering and tender.

"You wanted me to kiss you, too," he murmured against her lips.

A blush warmed her cheeks as she nodded. "It frightened me, how much I longed for it. Part of me thought I ought to run away, but your eyes..." She trailed off, her lashes lowering. "They held me captive, and I could not move."

His arms tightened as though he never wished to release her. "Then it seems I have discovered a most precious gift," he teased, his voice husky. "One I shall use whenever you think of running from me."

She laughed softly, though her heart pounded all the harder. When he lowered his lips to her ear, his breath warmed her skin, sending a delicious shiver down her spine.

"I love you, Sophie Everton," he whispered, each word weighted like a vow. Her breath caught, her eyes stung with sudden tears, and she nestled against him, overwhelmed by the strength of his love and the wonder of finally belonging in his arms.

Sophie stood before the Christmas tree, its branches glittering with ornaments and the warm glow of candles. The sight filled her heart with wonder. She could hardly believe it had been nearly two weeks since she had learned the truth—that Liam was not merely a wealthy stranger come to toy with her heart, but the Duke of Limerick himself. The memory still left her dizzy, though now her heart swelled with joy instead of disbelief.

She started when familiar arms slid gently around her waist.

Liam pressed a tender kiss to her cheek, and she instinctively leaned back against him, savoring his nearness.

"I have excellent news," he murmured warmly in her ear. "Your grandfather has agreed that once we're married, this house shall be ours. We can make it our country estate—a place of peace, beauty, and family."

Her eyes softened, though a crease lingered between her brows. "That would be wonderful, Liam, but what about my grandparents? Where will they live? Surely they cannot be sent away. I want them close."

Before Liam could respond, Augusta swept gracefully into the room, her smile as radiant as the morning sun.

"There is no need to worry, my dear. We'll have a smaller house built on this land for us. You and Liam deserve your own home to begin your lives together."

Edwin followed, nodding firmly. "Besides, matters are improving. Some of the funds we lent to help Albert have been returned. The tenants are coming back to our lands, including those who had been promised homes in Limerick. And," he added with quiet satisfaction, "we also received a portion of the reward money for aiding in the capture of Jack and Mable Murphy."

Sophie clasped her hands together, her eyes shining with relief. "That is splendid, Grandfather. I cannot tell you how happy it makes me to know all is being restored to you."

Edwin's stern features softened into a proud smile. "And until our new home is finished, we will stay with your Fitzpatrick grandparents. Delightful people, truly. They have decided to make Oaktree Castle their permanent residence instead of returning to Kilkenny. One of your grandfather's nephews, a marquess, will look after the duchy in their absence. They, like us, wish to remain close to their beloved granddaughter."

Sophie's throat tightened with emotion. For so long she had felt like an orphan, adrift without anchor. Now, at last, she was surrounded by love, belonging, and family on every side.

Liam lingered behind with Sophie as the others drifted toward the ballroom. He caught her hand, turning her gently to face him, his dark hazel eyes glowing with affection.

"Are you ready," he asked softly, "to be presented before society as the granddaughter of Lord Eamon Fitzpatrick, Duke of Kilkenny?"

Sophie bit her lip, then admitted shyly, "I am a little nervous."

His fingers closed around hers in a reassuring squeeze. "You need not be. You are already everything they could hope for, and more."

Before she could answer, Killian appeared, his ever-mischievous grin firmly in place. "And are you ready, Sophie, to become Lady Sophie Walsh, Duchess of Limerick, and my new sister tomorrow?"

Sophie turned at once, her gaze instinctively seeking Liam's. A smile broke across her face, radiant and full of quiet triumph.

"Yes, I am ready. And I believe, at last, I have fallen in love with the right brother."

Laughter rippled through the room, though Sophie scarcely heard it. Her eyes sparkled with such joy and devotion that Liam could not resist. He bent and kissed her—slow, passionate, and full of promise.

"One more day, Liam," came his father's teasing voice from the doorway. Lennon and Saoirse Walsh stepped into the room. "Don't lose your senses just yet, lad. Let the poor girl breathe."

With her cheeks aflame, Sophie buried her face against her fiancé's chest.

"You are incorrigible, Lennon," Saoirse scolded with a fond smile. "What a way to welcome Sophie into the family."

"She must learn quickly that Walshes are relentless teasers," Lennon said in mock solemnity, throwing his wife a daring look that made her laugh despite herself. Before their playful banter could continue, a servant's voice rang down the corridor, summoning them. The ballroom doors had opened, and the moment had come to present Sophie to the world—not as a captive, not as a girl without protection, but as a granddaughter, a marchioness, and a bride-to-be.

Eamon called Sophie to his side, his eyes alight with pride as he addressed the glittering crowd.

"May I present to you my granddaughter, Lady Sophie Aoife Everton Fitzpatrick, Marchioness of Kilkenny."

A swell of applause rose, warm and resounding, as Sophie felt herself embraced not only by her grandfather's arms but by the acceptance of every noble family gathered in the hall. Eamon pressed her close, his voice carrying once again.

"My apologies to any hopeful suitors," he teased, affection softening his tone, "but this young lady has already given her heart to an excellent young man, and I assure you, he is not willing to step aside."

Gentle laughter rippled through the ballroom while Sophie's cheeks flushed. Eamon then offered her his arm.

"May I have this dance, my darling girl?"

Sophie's eyes shone with tears she could scarcely contain. "You may, Grandfather."

The musicians struck up a graceful waltz as he led her onto the polished floor. In her grandfather's steady arms, Sophie moved as though she had been born for such a moment. Candlelit chandeliers glowed above them, the gilded walls reflecting the shimmer of jewels and silks.

"You are a wonderful dancer, Grandfather," Sophie said breathlessly. But when she looked up, she noticed his faraway gaze. "What are you thinking of? You look lost in thought."

His smile deepened, touched with emotion. "I was thinking how honored I am to be dancing with you. For years, your grandmother and I feared this day would never come. And yet, here you are—shining, loved, and free."

Overcome, Sophie rose on her tiptoes and pressed a tender kiss to his cheek. His answering smile brimmed with pride and love, and Sophie's throat tightened with more tears. She blinked them quickly away, unwilling to cloud the joy of the evening.

Minutes later, she was swept into the arms of her future husband. Liam's strong hands guided her with flawless ease as the waltz swirled around them. Every step, every turn seemed to echo the unspoken vow between them. Sophie could feel the weight of every gaze in the room, yet to her there was only him—the man who had risked everything, the man who had captured her heart.

Her pulse raced as he drew her closer, his breath brushing against her ear. She had thought nothing could rival the beauty of the candlelit ballroom, but she was wrong. Nothing was more beautiful than Liam's eyes as they rested on her, as though she were his entire world.

The whispers, the smiles, the approving glances of their families faded into nothing. There was no audience, no music, and no grandeur. Only the two of them, moving as one.

The following night, beneath a velvet sky scattered with stars, Liam carried his bride across the threshold of their home. The winter air was sharp and cold, but inside the drawing room a fire glowed low, waiting to be rekindled. The servants had departed to spend Christmas with their families, leaving the house pristine and hushed, as though it belonged to Sophie and Liam alone.

He set her gently on the settee before crossing to the hearth, where he laid fresh logs upon the embers. The flames leapt eagerly, casting golden warmth across the room. Sophie rose, her gown trailing behind her as she wandered to the Christmas tree. She reached to light one of the slender candles, but before her fingers touched the taper, Liam swept her into his arms.

Startled, she gasped softly, the sound melting into a breathless laugh as his gaze captured hers.

"The charm of Christmas makes our love all the more beautiful," he whispered, his voice low and reverent. His eyes lingered on the glowing tree before returning to her. "I am so glad your family chose this season for our wedding, for now Christmas will forever be ours."

Her cheeks warmed, her heart trembling as she met his gaze. Then his lips found hers. The kiss was deep and fervent, carrying both tenderness and promise, until Liam lowered himself onto the settee, never once loosening his embrace. Sophie melted against him, safe in the circle of his arms, her heartbeat finding its rhythm in his.

When at last their lips parted, Sophie nestled into his chest, her breath soft and content. "I love you, Liam," she whispered, her words trembling with truth.

"And I love you, Sophie." He pressed a lingering kiss into her hair, holding her as though he would never let her go. "Merry Christmas, my dearest. May our love burn brighter than any flame, endure every trial, and grow stronger with every passing year."

Sophie closed her eyes, her heart overflowing with joy, certain that this was only the beginning of a lifetime of love.

The End

Did you love *Her Hand in Marriage*? Then you should read *Kissed at Christmas Cottage*[1] by Rebecca Lange!

New Edition!!! - Released December 2025

A hidden truth. A devilishly handsome duke. A love caught between scandal and secrets.

Lady Ophelia Winter is content with her life—except for the name she despises and the endless suitors she rejects. Her father, the Viscount of Hethersett, is determined to see her wed, but Ophelia's stubborn independence leaves him exasperated.

But her world is thrown into turmoil when a letter exposes a shocking truth about her heritage, shattering everything she thought she knew. Struggling to accept her new reality, she soon clashes with the ton—especially over Lord Garrett Haywood, the Duke of Ashford. Devilishly handsome, rumored to be arrogant, and nearly engaged, he is everything she should resist... yet her heart refuses to obey.

When Ophelia defends a maid and overhears a dangerous conversation, she uncovers secrets that bind powerful families together. Suddenly, she is ensnared in a web of scandal and deceit—and marked as a target to be silenced.

About the Author

Rebecca Lange is a devoted romantic at heart. Though she has explored a variety of genres throughout her writing journey, her deepest passion lies in historical fiction—particularly stories set in the 1800s American West and the Regency era.

A passionate advocate, Rebecca uses her stories to raise awareness of abuse, human trafficking, and the devastating impact of drug and alcohol addiction. These themes are not woven in for suspense alone, but as a reminder that such struggles are tragically real—and that victims are never to blame.

She is also a firm believer in women's rights, inspired by the courageous women of the 1800s who fought to prove they were not the property of their husbands but their partners and equals. Rebecca upholds the conviction that violence has no place in relationships or marriage.

Originally from Germany, she was born and raised there before moving abroad in 2002 to serve a mission for her church in Scotland. A member of The Church of Jesus Christ of Latter-day Saints, she now lives in Utah with her husband, their two sons (ages 18 and 20), and two lively Yorkie puppies.

Her writing motto is: *Never Smut, Always Sizzling Kisses, Consistently Closed Door.* Rebecca delights in weaving passion and tenderness into her stories, offering what she calls "sweet and diet spice" romance. Diet spice—what is that, you ask? It's the thrill of longing gazes, passionate kisses, and close embraces that build anticipation without ever crossing into explicit territory. For her, the most powerful love stories are those that remain tasteful and teasing, proving that romance can be both heart-stirring and wholesome.

Read more at https://authorrebeccalange.wixsite.com/bookstolove.